'The BEST OF ...'
collections are intended to present the
representative stories of the masters of
science fiction in chronological order, their
aim being to provide science fiction readers
with a selection of short stories that
demonstrate the author's literary
development and at the same time providing
new readers with a sound introduction to
their work.

The collections were compiled with the help
and advice of the authors concerned,
together with the invaluable assistance of
numerous fans, without whose good work,
time and patience they would not have been
published.
In particular the advice of Roger Peyton,
Gerald Bishop, Peter Weston and Leslie
Flood is appreciated.

ANGUS WELLS, *Editor*, 1973

The Best of
Isaac Asimov
1954 – 1972

SPHERE BOOKS LIMITED
30/32 Gray's Inn Road, London WC1X 8JL

First published in Great Britain by Sphere Books Ltd 1977
Copyright © Isaac Asimov 1973
Anthology copyright © Sphere Books Ltd 1973
Introduction © Isaac Asimov 1973
Bibliography © Gerald Bishop 1973
Revised bibliography © Aardvark House 1977
Originally published in one volume entitled
THE BEST OF ISAAC ASIMOV

TRADE
MARK

Set in Linotype Times

Printed in Great Britain by
Hazell Watson & Viney Ltd
Aylesbury, Bucks

CONTENTS

Introduction	15
1954: The Fun They Had	18
1956: The Last Question	32
1956: The Dead Past	82
1956: The Dying Night	110
1959: Anniversary	127
1967: The Billiard Ball	148
1972: Mirror-Image	167
Bibliography	

ACKNOWLEDGEMENTS

The Fun They Had: *Fantasy & Science Fiction*, 1954
The Last Question: *Science Fiction Quarterly*, 1956
The Dead Past: *Astounding Science Fiction*, 1956
The Dying Night: *Fantasy & Science Fiction*, 1956
Anniversary: *Amazing Science Fiction*, 1959
The Billiard Ball: *If Science Fiction*, 1967
Mirror-Image: *Analog*, 1972

INTRODUCTION

I must admit the title of this book gives me pause. Who says the enclosed stories are my 'best'? Do I? Does the editor? Or some critic? Some reader? A general vote among the entire population of the United Kingdom? (Actually, it was the editor. I made some suggestions, but the final decision was his. Mr. Angus Wells is his name, if you have some stern comments to make.)

And whoever says it – can it be so? Can the word 'best' mean anything at all, except to some particular person in some particular mood? Perhaps not – so if we allow the word to stand as an absolute, you, or you, or perhaps you, may be appalled at omissions or inclusions or, never having read me before, may even be impelled to cry out, 'Good heavens, are *those* his *best*?'

So I'll be straight with all of you. What is included here in this book are a dozen stories chosen in such a way as to span a third a century of writing, with two early samples, two late samples, and eight from the gold decade (for me) of the Fifties. Those presented are as nearly representative as is consistent with the careful selection of good stories (i.e. those the editor and I like), and as nearly the best of my stories as is consistent with making them representative.

I suppose we ought really call the book, 'The Pretty Good and Pretty Representative Stories of Isaac Asimov', but who would then buy it? So 'Best' it is.

As to the individual stories –

(1) 'Marooned Off Vesta' was the very first story I ever published, so its inclusion is virtually a necessity. It wasn't the first story I ever wrote with the hope of publication. Actually, it was the third. The first was never

7

sold and no longer exists; the second was sold a couple of years after it was written, but is not very good.

Far be it from me to crave indulgence, but I think it is important to understand that at the time I wrote and sold the story (in 1938) I was eighteen years old and had spent all the years I could remember in a city-slum. My vision of strong adventurers bravely facing danger in distant vast-nesses was just that – visionary.

(2) 'Nightfall', written two and a half years later, was the thirty-second story I had written (what else did I have to do in those days except work in my father's candy-store – sweetshop, I think *you* call it – and study for my college degrees) and perhaps the fourteenth story pub-lished.

Yet within less than three years of the start of my career it turned out that I *had* written the best of Asimov. At least, 'Nightfall' has been frequently reprinted, is commonly referred to as a 'classic', and when some magazine, or fan organization, conducts a vote on short stories, it frequently ends up on the top of the list – not only of my stories but of anybody's. One of its advantages is that it has a unique plot. There was nothing resembling it ever published before (as far as I know) and of course, it is now so well known that nothing like it can be published again. It's nice to have *one* story like that, anyway.

Yet I was only twenty-one when I wrote it and was still feeling my way. It isn't *my* favorite. Later on, I'll tell you what my favorite is and you can then judge for yourself.

(3) 'C-Chute' comes after a ten-year hiatus, as far as the stories included in this book are concerned. I hadn't quit writing of course, don't think that. To be sure, I had slowed down a bit, what with the war and the time-consuming effort toward the doctorate, but the real reason for the gap is that I spent most of the Forties writing the stories collected in my books *I, Robot* and *The Foundation Trilogy*. It seemed inadvisable to amputate portions of either for this collec-tion.

'C-Chute' comes near the beginning of my 'mature' period (or whatever you want to call it). I had my Ph.D.; I was an Assistant Professor of Biochemistry at Boston University

School of Medicine; I had published my first three books; and I was full of self-confidence. What's more I had broken away from exclusive dependence on *Astounding Science Fiction*. New magazines had arisen to challenge its leadership, notably *Galaxy*, and also *Fantasy and Science Fiction*. 'C-Chute' appeared in *Galaxy*. So did the next two stories in the collection.

(4) 'The Martian Way' represents my reaction to what we in the United States call 'the McCarthy era', a time, in the early fifties, when Americans seemed to abandon their own history and become, in some cases, witch-hunters; in some cases, victims; and in most cases, cowards. (Brave men remained, fortunately, which is why we pulled out of it.) 'The Martian Way', written and published at the height of the McCarthy era, was my own personal statement of position. I felt very brave at the time and was disappointed that no one ever as much as frowned at me in consequence. I must have been too subtle – or too unimportant.

A second point about the story is that I managed to foresee something accurately. Science fiction writers are often assumed to be keen-eyed peerers-into-the-future who see things others don't. Actually, few writers have much of a record in this respect and mine, at best, can only be said to attain the abysmally-low average. Just the same, in 'The Martian Way', I described the euphoric effects of the space-walk fifteen years before anyone had space-walked – and then, when they did, euphoria is apparently what they experienced.

(5) 'The Deep' is the sleeper of the collection. Every once in a while I wrote a story which, though good in my opinion (and I don't like *all* my stories), seems to stir up no reaction. This is one of them. Perhaps it's because I deliberately chose to describe a society in which mother-love was a crime and the world wasn't ready for that.

(6) 'The Fun They Had' is probably the biggest surprise of my literary career. A personal friend asked me to write a little science fiction story for a syndicated boys-and-girls newspaper page he edited and I agreed for friendship's sake. I expected it would appear in a few newspapers for one day and would then disappear forever.

However, *Fantasy and Science Fiction* picked it up and, to my surprise, the reprint requests began to come in. It has been reprinted at least thirty times, and there has been no time in perhaps fifteen years (including right now) when new reprints haven't been pending.

Why? I don't know why. If I had the critic's mentality (which I emphatically don't) I would sit down and try to analyze my stories, work out the factors that make some more successful than others, cultivate those factors, and simply explode with excellence.

But the devil with that. I won't buy success at the price of self-consciousness. I don't have the temperament for it. I'll write as I please and let the critics do the analyzing. (Yesterday, someone said to me that a critic was like a eunuch in a harem. He could observe, study, and analyze – but he couldn't do it himself.)

(7) 'The Last Question' is my personal favourite, the one story I made sure would not be omitted from this collection.

Why is it my favorite? For one thing I got the idea all at once and didn't have to fiddle with it; and I wrote it in white-heat and scarcely had to change a word. This sort of thing endears any story to any writer.

Then, too, it has had the strangest effect on my readers. Frequently someone writes to ask me if I can give them the name of a story, which they *think* I may have written, and tell them where to find it. They don't remember the title but when they describe the story it is invariably 'The Last Question'. This has reached the point where I recently received a long-distance phone-call from a desperate man who began, 'Dr Asimov, there's a story I think you wrote, whose title I can't remember —' at which point I interrupted to tell him it was 'The Last Question' and when I described the plot it proved to be indeed the story he was after. I left him convinced I could read minds at a distance of a thousand miles.

No other story I have written has anything like this effect on my readers – producing at once an unshakeable memory of the plot and an unshakeable forgettery of the title and even author. I think it may be that the story fills them so frighteningly full, that they can retain none of the side-issues.

(8) 'The Dead Past' was written after I had been teaching for seven years. I was as saturated as could be with the world of scientific research.

Naturally, anyone who writes is going to reveal the world in which he is immersed, whether he wants to or desperately wants not to. I've never tried to avoid letting my personal background creep into my stories, but I must admit it has rarely crept in quite as thickly as it did in this one.

As an example of how my stories work out, consider this —

I had my protagonist interested in Carthage because I myself am a great admirer of Hannibal and have never quite gotten over the Battle of Zama. I introduced Carthage, idly, without any intention of weaving it into the plot. But it got woven in just the same.

That happens to me over and over. Some writers work out the stories in meticulous detail before starting, and stick to the outline. P. G. Wodehouse does it, I understand, and I worship his books. But just the same I don't. I work out my ending, decide on a beginning and then proceed, letting everything in-between work itself out as I come to it.

(9) 'The Dying Night' is an example of a mystery as well as a science fiction story. I have been a mystery reader as long as I have been a science fiction reader and, on the whole, I think I enjoy mysteries more.

I'm not sure why that is. Perhaps it was that after I became an established science fiction writer I was no longer able to relax with science fiction stories. I read every story keenly aware that it might be worse than mine, in which case I had no patience with it, or that it might be better, in which case I felt miserable.

Mysteries, especially the intellectual puzzle variety that English writers are so good at (ah, good old Hercule Poirot), offered me no such stumbling blocks. Sooner or later, then, I was bound to try my hand at science fiction mysteries and 'The Dying Night' is one of these.

(10) 'Anniversary', was written to fulfil a request – that I write a story for the March, 1959, issue of *Amazing Stories* as a way of celebrating the twentieth anniversary of the March, 1939, issue, which had contained my first published story, 'Marooned Off Vesta'. So (inevitably) I wrote a story dealing with the characters of 'Marooned Off Vesta' twenty years later. The magazine then ran both stories together, and I was sure someone would send me a letter saying that my writing was better in the first story, but no one did. (Perhaps a reader of this book will decide it would be humorous to do so, but if so, please restrain yourself.)

(11) 'The Billiard Ball' comes, in this collection, after an eight-year hiatus and is an example of my 'late' style. (That is, if there is such a thing. Some critics say that it is a flaw in my literary nature that I haven't 'grown'; that my late stories have the same style and aura of my early stories. Maybe you'll think so, too, and scorn me in consequence – but then, I've already told you what some people think of critics.)

The reason for the hiatus is that in 1958 I quit the academic life to become a full-time writer. I at once proceeded to write everything under the sun (straight science, straight mystery, children's books, histories, literary annotations, etymology, humor, etc., etc.) *except* science fiction. I never entirely abandoned it, of course – witness 'The Billiard Ball'.

(12) 'Mirror Image' is, to this date, the most recent science fiction short story I've written for the magazines and, unlike the first eleven stories, has never previously been reprinted.

One of the reasons for writing it was to appease those readers who were forever asking me for sequels; for one more book involving characters who have appeared in previous books. One of the most frequent requests was that I write a third novel to succeed *The Caves of Steel* and *The Naked Sun*, both of which dealt with the adventures of the detective, Elijah Baley, and his robot-assistant, R. Daneel Olivaw. Unable to find the time to do so, I wrote a short story about them – 'Mirror-Image'.

Alas, all I got as a result were a spate of letters saying, 'Thanks, but we mean a *novel*.'

Anyway, there you are. Turn the page and you can begin a representative, and possibly a more or less 'best', 100,000 words or so out of the roughly 2,000,000 words of science fiction I have written so far. I hope it amuses you. And if it doesn't, remember that I have also written about 7,500,000 words of *non*-science-fiction, and you are at least spared any of that.

ISAAC ASIMOV

MARGIE even wrote about it that night in her diary. On the page headed May 17, 2157, she wrote, 'Today Tommy found a real book!'

It was a very old book. Margie's grandfather once said that when he was a little boy *his* grandfather told him that there was a time when all stories were printed on paper.

They turned the pages, which were yellow and crinkly, and it was awfully funny to read words that stood still instead of moving the way they were supposed to – on a screen, you know. And then, when they turned back to the page before, it had the same words on it that it had had when they read it the first time.

'Gee,' said Tommy, 'what a waste. When you're through with the book, you just throw it away, I guess. Our television screen must have had a million books on it and it's good for plenty more. I wouldn't throw it away.'

'Same as mine,' said Margie. She was eleven and hadn't seen as many textbooks as Tommy had. He was thirteen.

She said, 'Where did you find it?'

'In my house.' He pointed without looking, because he was busy reading. 'In the attic.'

'What's it about?'

'School.'

Margie was scornful. 'School? What's there to write about school? I hate school.'

Margie always hated school, but now she hated it more than ever. The mechanical teacher had been giving her test after test in geography and she had been doing worse and worse until her mother had shaken her head sorrowfully and sent for the County Inspector.

He was a round little man with a red face and a whole box of tools with dials and wires. He smiled at Margie and gave her an apple, then took the teacher apart. Margie had hoped he wouldn't know how to put it together again, but he knew how all right, and, after an hour or so, there it was again, large and black and ugly, with a big screen on which all the lessons were shown and the questions were asked. That wasn't so bad. The part Margie hated most was the slot where she had to put homework and test papers. She always had to write them out in a punch code they made her learn when she was six years old, and the mechanical teacher calculated the mark in no time.

The Inspector had smiled after he was finished and patted Margie's head. He said to her mother, 'It's not the little girl's fault, Mrs. Jones. I think the geography sector was geared a little too quick. Those things happen sometimes. I've slowed it up to an average ten-year level. Actually, the over-all pattern of her progress is quite satisfactory.' And he patted Margie's head again.

Margie was disappointed. She had been hoping they would take the teacher away altogether. They had once taken Tommy's teacher away for nearly a month because the history sector had blanked out completely.

So she said to Tommy, 'Why would anyone write about school?'

Tommy looked at her with very superior eyes. 'Because it's not our kind of school, stupid. This is the old kind of school that they had hundreds and hundreds of years ago.' He added loftily, pronouncing the word carefully, 'Centuries ago.'

Margie was hurt. 'Well, I don't know what kind of school they had all that time ago.' She read the book over his shoulder for a while, then said, 'Anyway, they had a teacher.'

'Sure they had a teacher, but it wasn't a regular teacher. It was a man.'

'A man? How could a man be a teacher?'

'Well, he just told the boys and girls things and gave them homework and asked them questions.'

'A man isn't smart enough.'

'Sure he is. My father knows as much as my teacher.'

'He can't. A man can't know as much as a teacher.'

'He knows almost as much, I betcha.'

Margie wasn't prepared to dispute that. She said, 'I wouldn't want a strange man in my house to teach me.'

Tommy screamed with laughter. 'You don't know much,

Margie. The teachers didn't live in the house. They had a special building and all the kids went there.'

'And all the kids learned the same thing?'

'Sure, if they were the same age.'

'But my mother says a teacher has to be adjusted to fit the mind of each boy and girl it teaches and that each kid has to be taught differently.'

'Just the same they didn't do it that way then. If you don't like it, you don't have to read the book.'

'I didn't say I didn't like it,' Margie said quickly. She wanted to read about those funny schools.

They weren't even half-finished when Margie's mother called, 'Margie! School!'

Margie looked up. 'Not yet, Mamma.'

'Now!' said Mrs. Jones. 'And it's probably time for Tommy, too.'

Margie said to Tommy, 'Can I read the book some more with you after school?'

'Maybe,' he said nonchalantly. He walked away whistling, the dusty old book tucked beneath his arm.

Margie went into the schoolroom. It was right next to her bedroom, and the mechanical teacher was on and waiting for her. It was always on at the same time every day except Saturday and Sunday, because her mother said little girls learned better if they learned at regular hours.

The screen was lit up, and it said: 'Today's arithmetic lesson is on the addition of proper fractions. Please insert yesterday's homework in the proper slot.'

Margie did so with a sigh. She was thinking about the old schools they had when her grandfather's grandfather was a little boy. All the kids from the whole neighborhood came, laughing and shouting in the schoolyard, sitting together in the same schoolroom, going home together at the end of the day. They learned the same things, so they could help one another on the homework and talk about it.

And the teachers were people....

The mechanical teacher was flashing on the screen: 'When we add the fractions $\frac{1}{2}$ and $\frac{1}{4}$ —'

Margie was thinking about how the kids must have loved it in the old days. She was thinking about the fun they had.

THE LAST QUESTION

THE last question was asked for the first time, half in jest, on May 21, 2061, at a time when humanity first stepped into the light. The question came about as a result of a five-dollar bet over highballs, and it happened this way:

Alexander Adell and Bertram Lupov were two of the faithful attendants of Multivac. As well as any human beings could, they knew what lay behind the cold, clicking, flashing face – miles and miles of face – of that giant computer. They had at least a vague notion of the general plan of relays and circuits that had long since grown past the point where any single human could possibly have a firm grasp of the whole.

Multivac was self-adjusting and self-correcting. It had to be, for nothing human could adjust and correct it quickly enough or even adequately enough. – So Adell and Lupov attended the monstrous giant only lightly and superficially, yet as well as any men could. They fed it data, adjusted questions to its needs and translated the answers that were issued. Certainly they, and all others like them, were fully entitled to share in the glory that was Multivac's.

For decades, Multivac had helped design the ships and plot trajectories that enabled man to reach the Moon, Mars, and Venus, but past that, Earth's poor resources could not support the ships. Too much energy was needed for the long trips. Earth exploited its coal and uranium with increasing efficiency, but there was only so much of both.

But slowly Multivac learned enough to answer deeper questions more fundamentally, and on May 14, 2061, what had been theory, became fact.

The energy of the sun was stored, converted, and utilized directly on a planet-wide scale. All Earth turned off its burning coal, its fissioning uranium, and flipped the switch that connected all of it to a small station, one mile in diameter, circling the Earth at half the distance of the Moon. All Earth ran by invisible beams of sunpower.

Seven days had not sufficed to dim the glory of it and Adell and Lupov finally managed to escape from the public function, and to meet in quiet where no man would think of looking for them, in the deserted underground chambers, where portions of the mighty buried body of Multivac showed. Unattended, idling, sorting data with contented lazy clickings, Multivac, too, had earned its vacation and the boys appreciated that. They had no intention, originally, of disturbing it.

They had brought a bottle with them, and their only concern at the moment was to relax in the company of each other and the bottle.

'It's amazing when you think of it,' said Adell. His broad face had lines of weariness in it, and he stirred his drink slowly with a glass rod, watching the cubes of ice slur clumsily about. 'All the energy we can possibly ever use for free. Enough energy, if we wanted to draw on it, to melt all Earth into a big drop of impure liquid iron, and still never miss the energy so used. All the energy we could ever use, forever and forever and forever.'

Lupov cocked his head sideways. He had a trick of doing that when he wanted to be contrary, and he wanted to be contrary now, partly because he had had to carry the ice and glassware. 'Not forever,' he said.

'Oh hell, just about forever. Till the sun runs down, Bert.'

'That's not forever.'

'All right, then. Billions and billions of years. Twenty billion, maybe. Are you satisfied?'

Lupov put his fingers through his thinning hair as though to reassure himself that some was still left and sipped gently at his own drink. 'Twenty billion years isn't forever.'

'Well, it will last our time, won't it?'

'So would the coal and uranium.'

'All right, but now we can hook up each individual spaceship to the Solar Station, and it can go to Pluto and back a million times without every worrying about fuel. You can't do *that* on coal and uranium. Ask Multivac, if you don't believe me.'

'I don't have to ask Multivac. I know that.'

'Then stop running down what Multivac's done for us,'

said Adell, blazing up, 'It did all right.'

'Who says it didn't? What I say is that a sun won't last forever. That's all I'm saying. We're safe for twenty billion years, but then what?' Lupov pointed a slightly shaky finger at the other. 'And don't say we'll switch to another sun.'

There was silence for a while. Adell put his glass to his lips only occasionally, and Lupov's eyes slowly closed. They rested.

Then Lupov's eyes snapped open. 'You're thinking we'll switch to another sun when ours is done, aren't you?'

'I'm not thinking.'

'Sure you are. You're weak on logic, that's the trouble with you. You're like the guy in the story who was caught in a sudden shower and who ran to a grove of trees and got under one. He wasn't worried, you see, because he figured when one tree got wet through, he would just get under another one.'

'I get it,' said Adell. 'Don't shout. When the sun is done, the other stars will be gone, too.'

'Darn right they will,' muttered Lupov. 'It all had a beginning in the original cosmic explosion, whatever that was, and it'll all have an end when all the stars run down. Some run down faster than others. Hell, the giants won't last a hundred million years. The sun will last twenty billion years and maybe the dwarfs will last a hundred billion for all the good they are. But just give us a trillion years and everything will be dark. Entropy has to increase to maximum, that's all.'

'I know all about entropy,' said Adell, standing on his dignity.

'The hell you do.'

'I know as much as you do.'

'Then you know everything's got to run down someday.'

'All right. Who says they won't?'

'You did, you poor sap. You said we had all the energy we needed, forever. You said "forever".'

It was Adell's turn to be contrary. 'Maybe we can build things up again someday,' he said.

'Never.'

'Why not? Someday.'

'Never.'

'Ask Multivac.'

'*You* ask Multivac. I dare you. Five dollars says it can't be done.'

Adell was just drunk enough to try, just sober enough to be able to phrase the necessary symbols and operations into a question which, in words, might have corresponded to this: Will mankind one day without the net expediture of energy be able to restore the sun to its full youthfulness even after it had died of old age?

Or maybe it could be put more simply like this: How can the net amount of entropy of the universe be massively decreased?

Multivac fell dead and silent. The slow flashing of lights ceased, the distant sounds of clicking relays ended.

Then, just as the frightened technicians felt they could hold their breath no longer, there was a sudden springing to life of the teletype attached to that portion of Multivac. Five words were printed: INSUFFICIENT DATA FOR MEANINGFUL ANSWER.

'No bet,' whispered Lupov. They left hurriedly.

By next morning, the two, plagued with throbbing head and cottony mouth, had forgotten the incident.

Jerrodd, Jerrodine, and Jerrodette I and II watched the starry picture in the visiplate change as the passage through hyperspace was completed in its non-time lapse. At once, the even powdering of stars gave way to the predominance of a single bright marble-disk, centered.

'That's X-23,' said Jerrodd confidently. His thin hands clasped tightly behind his back and the knuckles whitened.

The little Jerrodettes, both girls, had experienced the hyperspace passage for the first time in their lives and were self-conscious over the momentary sensation of inside-outness. They buried their giggles and chased one another wildly about their mother, screaming, 'We've reached X-23 – we've reached X-23 – we've —'

'Quiet, children,' said Jerrodine sharply. 'Are you sure, Jerrodd?'

'What is there to be but sure?' asked Jerrodd, glancing up

at the bulge of featureless metal just under the ceiling. It ran the length of the room, disappearing through the wall at either end. It was as long as the ship.

Jerrodd scarcely knew a thing about the thick rod of metal except that it was called a Microvac, that one asked it questions if one wished; that if one did it still had its task of guiding the ship to a pre-ordered destination; of feeding on energies from the various Sub-galactic Power Stations; of computing the equations for the hyperspacial jumps.

Jerrodd and his family had only to wait and live in the comfortable residence quarters of the ship.

Someone had once told Jerrodd that the 'ac' at the end of 'Microvac' stood for 'analog computer' in ancient English, but he was on the edge of forgetting even that.

Jerrodine's eyes were moist as she watched the visiplate. 'I can't help it. I feel funny about leaving Earth.'

'Why, for Pete's sake?' demanded Jerrodd. 'We had nothing there. We'll have everything on X-23. You won't be alone. You won't be a pioneer. There are over a million people on the planet already. Good Lord, our great-grandchildren will be looking for new worlds because X-23 will be overcrowded.' Then, after a reflective pause, 'I tell you, it's a lucky thing the computers worked out interstellar travel the way the race is growing.'

'I know, I know,' said Jerrodine miserably.

Jerrodette I said promptly, 'Our Microvac is the best Microvac in the world.'

'I think so, too,' said Jerrodd, tousling her hair.

It *was* a nice feeling to have a Microvac of your own and Jerrodd was glad he was part of his generation and no other. In his father's youth, the only computers had been tremendous machines taking up a hundred square miles of land. There was only one to a planet. Planetary ACs they were called. They had been growing in size steadily for a thousand years and then, all at once, came refinement. In place of transistors, had come molecular valves so that even the largest Planetary AC could be put into a space only half the volume of a spaceship.

Jerrodd felt uplifted, as he always did when he thought that his own personal Microvac was many times more complicated than the ancient and primitive Multivac that had first tamed the Sun, and almost as complicated as Earth's Planetary AC (the largest) that had first solved the problem of hyperspatial travel and had made trips to the stars possible.

'So many stars, so many planets,' sighed Jerrodine, busy with her own thoughts. 'I suppose families will be going out to new planets forever, the way we are now.'

'Not forever,' said Jerrodd, with a smile. 'It will all stop someday, but not for billions of years. Many billions. Even the stars run down, you know. Entropy must increase.'

'What's entropy, daddy?' shrilled Jerrodette II.

'Entropy, little sweet, is just a word which means the amount of running-down of the universe. Everything runs down, you know, like your little walkie-talkie robot, remember?'

'Can't you just put in a new power-unit, like with my robot?'

'The stars *are* the power-units, dear. Once they're gone, there are no more power-units.'

Jerrodette I at once set up a howl. 'Don't let them, daddy. Don't let the stars run down.'

'Now look what you've done,' whispered Jerrodine, exasperated.

'How was I to know it would frighten them?' Jerrodd whispered back.

'Ask the Microvac,' wailed Jerrodette I. 'Ask him how to turn the stars on again.'

'Go ahead,' said Jerrodine. 'It will quiet them down.' (Jerrodette II was beginning to cry, also.)

Jerrodd shrugged. 'Now, now, honeys. I'll ask Microvac. Don't worry, he'll tell us.'

He asked the Microvac, adding quickly, 'Print the answer.'

Jerrodd cupped the strip of thin cellufilm and said cheerfully, 'See now, the Microvac says it will take care of everything when the time comes so don't worry.'

Jerrodine said, 'And now, children, it's time for bed. We'll be in our new home soon.'

Jerrodd read the words on the cellufilm again before

23

destroying it: INSUFFICIENT DATA FOR MEANINGFUL ANSWER.

He shrugged and looked at the visiplate. X-23 was just ahead.

VJ-23X of Lameth stared into the black depths of the three-dimensional, small-scale map of the Galaxy and said, 'Are we ridiculous, I wonder, in being so concerned about the matter?'

MQ-17J of Nicron shook his head. 'I think not. You know the Galaxy will be filled in five years at the present rate of expansion.'

Both seemed in their early twenties, both were tall and perfectly formed.

'Still,' said VJ-23X, 'I hesitate to submit a pessimistic report to the Galactic Council.'

'I wouldn't consider any other kind of report. Stir them up a bit. We've got to stir them up.'

VJ-23X sighed. 'Space is infinite. A hundred billion Galaxies are there for the taking. More.'

'A hundred billion is *not* infinite and it's getting less infinite all the time. Consider! Twenty thousand years ago, mankind first solved the problem of utilizing stellar energy, and a few centuries later, interstellar travel became possible. It took mankind a million years to fill one small world and then only fifteen thousand years to fill the rest of the Galaxy. Now the population doubles every ten years —'

VJ-23X interrupted. 'We can thank immortality for that.'

'Very well. Immortality exists and we have to take it into account. I admit it has its seamy side, this immortality. The Galactic AC has solved many problems for us, but in solving the problem of preventing old age and death, it has undone all its other solutions.'

'Yet you wouldn't want to abandon life, I suppose.'

'Not at all,' snapped MQ-17J, softening it at once to, 'Not yet. I'm by no means old enough. How old are you?'

'Two hundred twenty-three. And you?'

'I'm still under two hundred. But to get back to my point. Population doubles every ten years. Once this Galaxy is filled, we'll have filled another in ten years. Another ten years and we'll have filled two more. Another decade, four

24

more. In a hundred years, we'll have filled a thousand Galaxies. In a thousand years, a million Galaxies. In ten thousand years, the entire known Universe. Then what?'

VJ-23X said, 'As a side issue, there's a problem of transportation. I wonder how many sunpower units it will take to move Galaxies of individuals from one Galaxy to the next.'

'A very good point. Already, mankind consumes two sunpower units per year.'

'Most of it's wasted. After all, our own Galaxy alone pours out a thousand sunpower units a year and we only use two of those.'

'Granted, but even with a hundred per cent efficiency, we only stave off the end. Our energy requirements are going up in a geometric progression even faster than our population. We'll run out of energy even sooner than we run out of Galaxies. A good point. A very good point.'

'We'll just have to build new stars out of interstellar gas.'

'Or out of dissipated heat?' asked MQ-17J, sarcastically.

'There may be some way to reverse entropy. We ought to ask the Galactic AC.'

VJ-23X was not really serious, but MQ-17J pulled out his AC-contact from his pocket and placed it on the table before him.

'I've half a mind to,' he said. 'It's something the human race will have to face someday.'

He stared somberly at his small AC-contact. It was only two inches cubed and nothing in itself, but it was connected through hyperspace with the great Galactic AC that served all mankind. Hyperspace considered, it was an integral part of the Galactic AC.

MQ-17J paused to wonder if someday in his immortal life he would get to see the Galactic AC. It was on a little world of its own, a spider webbing of force-beams holding the matter within which surges of sub-mesons took the place of the old clumsy molecular valves. Yet despite its sub-etheric workings, the Galactic AC was known to be a full thousand feet across.

MQ-17J asked suddenly of his AC-contact, 'Can entropy ever be reversed?'

VJ-23X looked startled and said at once, 'Oh, say, I

didn't really mean to have you ask that.'

'Why not?'

'We both know entropy can't be reversed. You can't turn smoke and ash back into a tree.'

'Do you have trees on your world?' asked MQ-17J.

The sound of the Galactic AC startled them into silence. Its voice came thin and beautiful out of the small AC-contact on the desk. It said: THERE IS INSUFFICIENT DATA FOR A MEANINGFUL ANSWER.

VJ-23X said, 'See!'

The two men thereupon returned to the question of the report they were to make to the Galactic Council.

Zee Prime's mind spanned the new Galaxy with a faint interest in the countless twists of stars that powdered it. He had never seen this one before. Would he ever see them all? So many of them, each with its load of humanity. But a load that was almost a dead weight. More and more, the real essence of men was to be found out here, in space.

Minds, not bodies! The immortal bodies remained back on the planets, in suspension over the eons. Sometimes they roused for material activity but that was growing rarer. Few new individuals were coming into existence to join the incredibly mighty throng, but what matter? There was little room in the Universe for new individuals.

Zee Prime was roused out of his reverie upon coming across the wispy tendrils of another mind.

'I am Zee Prime,' said Zee Prime. 'And you?'

'I am Dee Sub Wun. Your Galaxy?'

'We call it only the Galaxy. And you?'

'We call ours the same. All men call their Galaxy their Galaxy and nothing more. Why not?'

'True. Since all Galaxies are the same.'

'Not all Galaxies. On one particular Galaxy the race of man must have originated. That makes it different.'

Zee Prime said, 'On which one?'

'I cannot say. The Universal AC would know.'

'Shall we ask him? I am suddenly curious.'

Zee Prime's perceptions broadened until the Galaxies themselves shrank and became a new, more diffuse powdering on a much larger background. So many hundreds of billions of them, all with their immortal beings, all carrying their load of intelligences with minds that drifted freely through space. And yet one of them was unique among them all in being the original Galaxy. One of them had, in its vague and distant past, a period when it was the only Galaxy populated by man.

Zee Prime was consumed with curiosity to see this Galaxy and he called out : 'Universal AC! On which Galaxy did mankind originate?'

The Universal AC heard, for on every world and throughout space, it had its receptors ready, and each receptor lead through hyperspace to some unknown point where the Universal AC kept itself aloof.

Zee Prime knew of only one man whose thoughts had penetrated within sensing distance of Universal AC, and he reported only a shining globe, two feet across, difficult to see.

'But how can that be all of Universal AC?' Zee Prime had asked.

'Most of it,' had been the answer 'is in hyperspace. In what form it is there I cannot imagine.'

Nor could anyone, for the day had long since passed, Zee Prime knew, when any man had any part of the making of a Universal AC. Each Universal AC designed and constructed its successor. Each, during its existence of a million years or more accumulated the necessary data to build a better and more intricate, more capable successor in which its own store of data and individuality would be submerged.

The Universal AC interrupted Zee Prime's wandering thoughts, not with words, but with guidance. Zee Prime's mentality was guided into the dim sea of Galaxies and one in particular enlarged into stars.

A thought came, infinitely distant, but infinitely clear. 'THIS IS THE ORIGINAL GALAXY OF MAN.'

But it was the same after all, the same as any other, and Zee Prime stifled his disappointment.

Dee Sub Wun, whose mind had accompanied the other, said suddenly, 'And is one of these stars the original star of Man?'

The Universal AC said, 'MAN'S ORIGINAL STAR HAS GONE NOVA. IT IS A WHITE DWARF.'

'Did the men upon it die?' asked Zee Prime, startled and without thinking.

The Universal AC said, 'A NEW WORLD, AS IN SUCH CASES, WAS CONSTRUCTED FOR THEIR PHYSICAL BODIES IN TIME.'

'Yes, of course,' said Zee Prime, but a sense of loss overwhelmed him even so. His mind released its hold on the original Galaxy of Man, let it spring back and lose itself among the blurred pin points. He never wanted to see it again.

Dee Sub Wun said, 'What is wrong?'

'The stars are dying. The original star is dead.'

'They must all die. Why not?'

'But when all energy is gone, our bodies will finally die, and you and I with them.'

'It will take billions of years.'

'I do not wish it to happen even after billions of years. Universal AC! How may stars be kept from dying?'

Dee Sub Wun said in amusement, 'You're asking how entropy might be reversed in direction.'

And the Universal AC answered: 'THERE IS AS YET INSUFFICIENT DATA FOR A MEANINGFUL ANSWER.'

Zee Prime's thoughts fled back to his own Galaxy. He gave no further thought to Dee Sub Wun, whose body might be waiting on a Galaxy a trillion light-years away, or on the star next to Zee Prime's own. It didn't matter.

Unhappily, Zee Prime began collecting interstellar hydrogen out of which to build a small star of his own. If the stars must someday die, at least some could yet be built.

Man considered with himself, for in a way, Man, mentally, was one. He consisted of a trillion, trillion, trillion ageless bodies, each in its place, each resting quiet and incorruptible, each cared for by perfect automatons, equally incorruptible, while the minds of all the bodies freely melted one into the other, indistinguishable.

Man said, 'The Universe is dying.'

Man looked about at the dimming Galaxies. The giant stars, spendthrifts, were gone long ago, back in the dimmest of the dim far past. Almost all stars were white dwarfs, fading to the end.

New stars had been built of the dust between the stars, some by natural processes, some by Man himself, and those were going, too. White dwarfs might yet be crashed together and of the mighty forces so released, new stars built, but only one star for every thousand white dwarfs destroyed, and those would come to an end, too.

Man said, 'Carefully husbanded, as directed by the Cosmic AC, the energy that is even yet left in all the Universe will last for billions of years.'

'But even so,' said Man, 'eventually it will all come to an end. However it may be husbanded, however stretched out, the energy once expended is gone and cannot be restored. Entropy must increase forever to the maximum.'

Man said, 'Can entropy not be reversed? Let us ask the Cosmic AC.'

The Cosmic AC surrounded them but not in space. Not a fragment of it was in space. It was in hyperspace and made of something that was neither matter nor energy. The question of its size and nature no longer had meaning in any terms that Man could comprehend.

'Cosmic AC,' said Man, 'how may entropy be reversed?'

The Cosmic AC said, 'THERE IS AS YET INSUFFICIENT DATA FOR A MEANINGFUL ANSWER.'

Man said, 'Collect additional data.'

The Cosmic AC said, 'I WILL DO SO. I HAVE BEEN DOING SO FOR A HUNDRED BILLION YEARS. MY PREDECESSORS AND I HAVE BEEN ASKED THIS QUESTION MANY TIMES. ALL THE DATA I HAVE REMAINS INSUFFICIENT.'

'Will there come a time,' said Man, 'when data will be sufficient or is the problem insoluble in all conceivable circumstances?'

The Cosmic AC said, 'NO PROBLEM IS INSOLUBLE IN ALL CONCEIVABLE CIRCUMSTANCES.'

Man said, 'When will you have enough data to answer the question?'

The Cosmic AC said, 'THERE IS AS YET INSUFFICIENT DATA FOR A MEANINGFUL ANSWER.'

'Will you keep working on it?' asked Man.

The Cosmic AC said, 'I WILL.'

Man said, 'We shall wait.'

The stars and Galaxies died and snuffed out, and space grew black after ten trillion years of running down.

One by one Man fused with AC, each physical body losing its mental identity in a manner that was somehow not a loss but a gain.

Man's last mind paused before fusion, looking over a space that included nothing but the dregs of one last dark star and nothing besides but incredibly thin matter, agitated randomly by the tag ends of heat wearing out, asymptotically, to the absolute zero.

Man said, 'AC, is this the end? Can this chaos not be reversed into the Universe once more? Can that not be done?'

AC said, 'THERE IS AS YET INSUFFICIENT DATA FOR A MEANINGFUL ANSWER.'

Man's last mind fused and only AC existed – and that in hyperspace.

Matter and energy had ended and with it space and time. Even AC existed only for the sake of the one last question that it had never answered from the time a half-drunken computer ten trillion years before had asked the question of a computer that was to AC far less than was a man to Man.

All other questions had been answered, and until this last question was answered also, AC might not release his consciousness.

All collected data had come to a final end. Nothing was left to be collected.

But all collected data had yet to be completely correlated and put together in all possible relationships.

A timeless interval was spent in doing that.

And it came to pass that AC learned how to reverse the direction of entropy.

But there was now no man to whom AC might give the answer of the last question. No matter. The answer – by demonstration – would take care of that, too.

For another timeless interval, AC thought how best to do this. Carefully, AC organized the program.

The consciousness of AC encompassed all of what had once been a Universe and brooded over what was now Chaos. Step by step, it must be done.

And AC said, 'LET THERE BE LIGHT!'

And there was light —

THE DEAD PAST

ARNOLD POTTERLEY, Ph.D., was a Professor of Ancient History. That, in itself, was not dangerous. What changed the world beyond all dreams was the fact that he *looked* like a Professor of Ancient History.

Thaddeus Araman, Department Head of the Division of Chronoscopy, might have taken proper action if Dr. Potterley had been owner of a large, square chin, flashing eyes, aquiline nose and broad shoulders.

As it was, Thaddeus Araman found himself staring over his desk at a mild-mannered individual, whose faded blue eyes looked at him wistfully from either side of a low-bridged button nose; whose small, neatly dressed figure seemed stamped 'milk-and-water' from thinning brown hair to the neatly brushed shoes that completed a conservative middle-class costume.

Araman said pleasantly, 'And now what can I do for you, Dr. Potterley?'

Dr. Potterley said in a soft voice that went well with the rest of him, 'Mr. Araman, I came to you because you're top man in chronoscopy.'

Araman smiled. 'Not exactly. Above me is the World Commissioner of Research and above him is the Secretary-General of the United Nations. And above both of them, of course, are the sovereign peoples of Earth.'

Dr. Potterley shook his head. 'They're not interested in chronoscopy. I've come to you, sir, because for two years I have been trying to obtain permission to do some time viewing – chronoscopy, that is – in connection with my researches on ancient Carthage. I can't obtain such permission. My research grants are all proper. There is no irregularity in any of my intellectual endeavors and yet —'

'I'm sure there is no question of irregularity,' said Araman soothingly. He flipped the thin reproduction sheets in the folder to which Potterley's name had been attached.

They had been produced by Multivac, whose vast analogical mind kept all the department records. When this was over, the sheets could be destroyed, then reproduced on demand in a matter of minutes.

And while Araman turned the pages, Dr. Potterley's voice continued in a soft monotone.

The historian was saying, 'I must explain that my problem is quite an important one. Carthage was ancient commercialism brought to its zenith. Pre-Roman Carthage was the nearest ancient analogue to pre-atomic America, at least insofar as its attachment to trade, commerce and business in general was concerned. They were the most daring seamen and explorers before the Vikings; much better at it than the overrated Greeks.

'To know Carthage would be very rewarding, yet the only knowledge we have of it is derived from the writings of its bitter enemies, the Greeks and Romans. Carthage itself never wrote in its own defense or, if it did, the books did not survive. As a result, the Carthaginians have been one of the favorite sets of villains of history and perhaps unjustly so. Time viewing may set the record straight.'

He said much more.

Araman said, still turning the reproduction sheets before him, 'You must realize, Dr. Potterley, that chronoscopy, or time viewing, if you prefer, is a difficult process.'

Dr. Potterley, who had been interrupted, frowned and said, 'I am asking for only certain selected views at times and places I would indicate.'

Araman sighed. 'Even a few views, even one ... It is an unbelievably delicate art. There is the question of focus, getting the proper scene in view and holding it. There is the synchronization of sound, which calls for completely independent circuits.'

'Surely my problem is important enough to justify considerable effort.'

'Yes, sir. Undoubtedly,' said Araman at once. To deny the importance of someone's research problem would be unforgivably bad manners. 'But you must understand how long-drawn-out even the simplest view is. And there is a long waiting line for the chronoscope and an even longer waiting line for the use of Multivac which guides us in our use of the controls.'

Potterley stirred unhappily. 'But can nothing be done? For two years —'

'A matter of priority, sir. I'm sorry.... Cigarette?'

The historian started back at the suggestion, eyes suddenly widening as he stared at the pack thrust out toward him. Araman looked surprised, withdrew the pack, made a motion as though to take a cigarette for himself and thought better of it.

Potterley drew a sigh of unfeigned relief as the pack was put out of sight. He said, 'Is there any way of reviewing matters, putting me as far forward as possible. I don't know how to explain —'

Araman smiled. Some had offered money under similar circumstances which, of course, had gotten them nowhere, either. He said, 'The decisions on priority are computer-processed. I could in no way alter those decisions arbitrarily.'

Potterley rose stiffly to his feet. He stood five and a half feet tall. 'Then, good day, sir.'

'Good day, Dr. Potterley. And my sincerest regrets.'

He offered his hand and Potterley touched it briefly.

The historian left, and a touch of the buzzer brought Araman's secretary into the room. He handed her the folder.

'These,' he said, 'may be disposed of.'

Alone again, he smiled bitterly. Another item in his quarter-century's service to the human race. Service through negation.

At least this fellow had been easy to dispose of. Sometimes academic pressure had to be applied and even withdrawal of grants.

Five minutes later, he had forgotten Dr. Potterley. Nor, thinking back on it later, could he remember feeling any premonition of danger.

During the first year of his frustration, Arnold Potterley had experienced only that – frustration. During the second year, though, his frustration gave birth to an idea that first frightened and then fascinated him. Two things stopped him from trying to translate the idea into action, and neither barrier was the undoubted fact this his notion was a grossly unethical one.

The first was merely the continuing hope that the government would finally give its permission and make it unnecessary for him to do anything more. That hope had perished finally in the interview with Araman just completed.

The second barrier had been not a hope at all but a dreary realization of his own incapacity. He was not a physicist and he knew no physicists from whom he might obtain help. The Department of Physics at the university consisted of men well stocked with grants and well immersed in specialty. At best, they would not listen to him. At worst, they would report him for intellectual anarchy and even his basic Carthaginian grant might easily be withdrawn.

That he could not risk. And yet chronoscopy was the only way to carry on his work. Without it, he would be no worse off if his grant were lost.

The first hint that the second barrier might be overcome had come a week earlier than his interview with Araman, and it had gone unrecognized at the time. It had been at one of the faculty teas. Potterley attended these sessions unfailingly because he conceived attendance to be a duty, and he took his duties seriously. Once there, however, he conceived it to be no responsibility of his to make light conversation or new friends. He sipped abstemiously at a drink or two, exchanging a polite word with the dean or such department heads as happened to be present, bestowed a narrow smile on others and finally left early.

Ordinarily, he would have paid no attention, at that most recent tea, to a young man standing quietly, even diffidently, in one corner. He would never have dreamed of speaking to him. Yet a tangle of circumstances persuaded him this once to behave in a way contrary to his nature.

That morning at breakfast, Mrs. Potterley had announced somberly that once again she had dreamed of Laurel, but this time a Laurel grown up, yet retaining the three-year-old face that stamped her as their child. Potterley had let her talk. There had been a time when he fought her too frequent

35

preoccupation with the past and death. Laurel would not come back to them, either through dreams or through talk. Yet if it appeased Caroline Potterley – let her dream and talk.

But when Potterley went to school that morning, he found himself for once affected by Caroline's inanities. Laurel grown up! She had died nearly twenty years ago; their only child, then and ever. In all that time, when he thought of her, it was as a three-year-old.

Now he thought: But if she were alive now, she wouldn't be three, she'd be nearly twenty-three.

Helplessly, he found himself trying to think of Laurel as growing progressively older; as finally becoming twenty-three. He did not quite succeed.

Yet he tried. Laurel using make-up. Laurel going out with boys. Laurel – getting married!

So it was that when he saw the young man hovering at the outskirts of the coldly circulating group of faculty men, it occurred to him quixotically that, for all he knew, a youngster just such as this might have married Laurel. That youngster himself, perhaps. . . .

Laurel might have met him, here at the university, or some evening when he might be invited to dinner at the Potterleys'. They might grow interested in one another. Laurel would surely have been pretty and this youngster looked well. He was dark in coloring, with a lean face and an easy carriage.

The tenuous daydream snapped, yet Potterley found himself staring foolishly at the young man, not as a strange face but as a possible son-in-law in the might-have-been. He found himself threading his way toward the man. It was almost a form of autohypnotism.

He put out his hand. 'I am Arnold Potterley of the History Department. You're new here, I think?'

The youngster looked faintly astonished and fumbled with his drink, shifting it to his left hand in order to shake with his right. 'Jonas Foster is my name, sir. I'm a new instructor in physics. I'm just starting this semester.'

Potterley nodded. 'I wish you a happy stay here and great success.'

That was the end of it, then. Potterley had come uneasily to his senses, found himself embarrassed and moved off. He stared back over his shoulder once, but the illusion of relationship had gone. Reality was quite real once more and he was angry with himself for having fallen prey to his wife's foolish talk about Laurel.

But a week later, even while Araman was talking, the thought of that young man had come back to him. An instructor in physics. A new instructor. Had he been deaf at the time? Was there a short circuit between ear and brain? Or was it an automatic self-censorship because of the impending interview with the Head of Chronoscopy?

But the interview failed, and it was the thought of the young man with whom he had exchanged two sentences that prevented Potterley from elaborating his pleas for consideration. He was almost anxious to get away.

And in the autogiro express back to the university, he could almost wish he were superstitious. He could then console himself with the thought that the casual meaningless meeting had really been directed by a knowing and purposeful Fate.

Jonas Foster was not new to academic life. The long and rickety struggle for the doctorate would make anyone a veteran. Additional work as a postdoctorate teaching fellow acted as a booster shot.

But now he was Instructor Jonas Foster. Professional dignity lay ahead. And he now found himself in a new sort of relationship toward other professors.

For one thing, they would be voting on future promotions. For another, he was in no position to tell so early in the game which particular member of the faculty might or might not have the ear of the dean or even of the university president. He did not fancy himself as a campus politician and was sure he would make a poor one, yet there was no point in kicking his own rear into blisters just to prove that to himself.

So Foster listened to this mild-mannered historian who, in some vague way, seemed nevertheless to radiate tension, and did not shut him up abruptly and toss him out. Cer-

37

tainly that was his first impulse.

He remembered Potterley well enough. Potterley had approached him at that tea (which had been a grizzly affair). The fellow had spoken two sentences to him stiffly, somehow glassy-eyed, had then come to himself with a visible start and hurried off.

It had amused Foster at the time, but now ...

Potterley might have been deliberately trying to make his acquaintance, or, rather, to impress his own personality on Foster as that of a queer sort of duck, eccentric but harmless. He might now be probing Foster's views, searching for unsettling opinions. Surely, they ought to have done so before granting him his appointment. Still ...

Potterley might be serious, might honestly not realize what he was doing. Or he might realize quite well what he was doing; he might be nothing more or less than a dangerous rascal.

Foster mumbled, 'Well now —' to gain time, and fished out a package of cigarettes, intending to offer one to Potterley and to light it and one for himself very slowly.

But Potterley said at once, 'Please, Dr. Foster. No cigarettes.'

Foster looked startled. 'I'm sorry, sir.'

'No. The regrets are mine. I cannot stand the odour. An idiosyncrasy, I'm sorry.'

He was positively pale. Foster put away the cigarettes.

Foster, feeling the absence of the cigarette, took the easy way out. 'I'm flattered that you ask my advice and all that, Dr. Potterley, but I'm not a neutrinics man. I can't very well do anything professional in that direction. Even stating an opinion would be out of line, and, frankly, I'd prefer that you didn't go into any particulars.'

The historian's prim face set hard. 'What do you mean, you're not a neutrinics man? You're not anything yet. You haven't received any grant, have you?'

'This is only my first semester.'

'I know that. I imagine you haven't even applied for any grant yet.'

Foster half-smiled. In three months at the university, he had not succeeded in putting his initial requests for research grants into good enough shape to pass on to a professional science writer, let alone to the Research Commission.

(His Department Head, fortunately, took it quite well. 'Take your time now, Foster,' he said, 'and get your thoughts well organized. Make sure you know your path and where it will lead, for, once you receive a grant, your specialization will be formally recognized and, for better or for worse, it will be yours for the rest of your career.' The advice was trite enough, but triteness has often the merit of truth, and Foster recognized that.)

Foster said, 'By education and inclination, Dr. Potterley, I'm a hyperoptics man with a gravitics minor. It's how I described myself in applying for this position. It may not be my official specialization yet, but it's going to be. It can't be anything else. As for neutrinics, I never even studied the subject.'

'Why not!' demanded Potterley at once.

Foster stared. It was the kind of rude curiosity about another man's professional status that was always irritating. He said, with the edge of his own politeness just a trifle blunted, 'A course in neutrinics wasn't given at my university.'

'Good Lord, where did you go?'

'M.I.T.,' said Foster quietly.

'And they don't teach neutrinics?'

'No, they don't.' Foster felt himself flush and was moved to a defense. 'It's a highly specialized subject with no great value. Chronoscopy, perhaps, has some value, but it is the only practical application and that's a dead end.'

The historian stared at him earnestly. 'Tell me this. Do you know where I can find a neutrinics man?'

'No, I don't;' said Foster bluntly.

'Well, then, do you know a school which teaches neutrinics?'

'No, I don't.'

Potterley smiled tightly and without humour.

Foster resented that smile, found he detected insult in it and grew sufficiently annoyed to say, 'I would like to point out, sir, that you're stepping out of line.'

'What?'

'I'm saying that, as a historian, your interest in any sort of physics, your *professional* interest, is —' He paused, unable to bring himself quite to say the word.

'Unethical?'

'That's the word, Dr. Potterley.'

'My researches have driven me to it,' said Potterley in an intense whisper.

'The Research Commission is the place to go. If they permit —'

'I have gone to them and have received no satisfaction.'

'Then obviously you must abandon this.' Foster knew he was sounding stuffily virtuous, but he wasn't going to let this man lure him into an expression of intellectual anarchy. It was too early in his career to take stupid risks.

Apparently, though, the remark had its effect on Potterley. Without any warning, the man exploded into a rapid-fire verbal storm of irresponsibility.

Scholars, he said, could be free only if they could freely follow their own free-swinging curiosity. Research, he said, forced into a predesigned pattern by the powers that held the purse strings became slavish and had to stagnate. No man, he said, had the right to dictate the intellectual interests of another.

Foster listened to all of it with disbelief. None of it was strange to him. He had heard college boys talk so in order to shock their professors and he had once or twice amused himself in that fashion, too. Anyone who studied the history of science knew that many men had once thought so.

Yet it seemed strange to Foster, almost against nature, that a modern man of science could advance such nonsense. No one would advocate running a factory by allowing each individual worker to do whatever pleased him at the moment, or running a ship according to the casual and conflicting notions of each individual crewman. It would be taken for granted that some sort of centralized supervisory agency must exist in each case. Why should direction and order benefit a factory and a ship but not scientific research?

People might say that the human mind was somehow qualitatively different from a ship or factory but the history of intellectual endeavor proved the opposite.

When science was young and the intricacies of all or most of the known was within the grasp of an individual mind, there was no need for direction, perhaps. Blind wandering over the uncharted tracts of ignorance could lead to wonderful finds by accident.

But as knowledge grew, more and more data had to be absorbed before worthwhile journeys into ignorance could be organized. Men had to specialize. The researcher needed the resources of a library he himself could not gather, then of instruments he himself could not afford. More and more, the individual researcher gave way to the research team and the research institution.

The funds necessary for research grew greater as tools grew more numerous. What college was so small today as not to require at least one nuclear micro-reactor and at least one three-stage computer?

Centuries before, private individuals could no longer subsidize research. By 1940, only the government, large industries and large universities or research institutions could properly subsidize basic research.

By 1960, even the largest universities depended entirely upon government grants, while research institutions could not exist without tax concessions and public subscriptions. By 2000, the industrial combines had become a branch of the world government and, thereafter, the financing of research and therefore its direction naturally became centralized under a department of the government.

It all worked itself out naturally and well. Every branch of science was fitted neatly to the needs of the public, and the various branches of science were co-ordinated decently. The material advance of the last half-century was argument enough for the fact that science was not falling into stagnation.

Foster tried to say a very little of this and was waved aside impatiently by Potterley who said, 'You are parroting official propaganda. You're sitting in the middle of an example that's squarely against the official view. Can you believe that?'

'Frankly, no?'

'Well, why do you say time viewing is a dead end? Why

41

is neutrinics unimportant? You say it is. You say it categorically. Yet you've never studied it. You claim complete ignorance of the subject. It's not even given in your school —'

'Isn't the mere fact that it isn't given proof enough?'

'Oh, I see. It's not given because it's unimportant. And it's unimportant because it's not given. Are you satisfied with that reasoning?'

Foster felt a growing confusion. 'It's in the books.'

'That's all. The books say neutrinics is unimportant. Your professors tell you so because they read it in the books. The books say so because professors write them. Who says it from personal experience and knowledge? Who does research in it? Do you know anyone?'

Foster said, 'I don't see that we're getting anywhere, Dr. Potterley. I have work to do —'

'One minute. I just want you to try this on. See how it sounds to you. I say the government is actively suppressing basic research in neutrinics and chronoscopy. They're suppressing application of chronoscopy.'

'Oh no.'

'Why not? They could do it. There's your centrally directed research. If they refuse grants for research in any portion of science, that portion dies. They've killed neutrinics. They can do it and have done it.'

'But why?'

'I don't know why. I want you to find out. I'd do it myself if I knew enough. I came to you because you're a young fellow with a brand-new education. Have your intellectual arteries hardened already? Is there no curiosity in you? Don't you want to *know*? Don't you want *answers*?'

The historian was peering intently into Foster's face. Their noses were only inches apart, and Foster was so lost that he did not think to draw back.

He should, by rights, have ordered Potterley out. If necessary, he should have thrown Potterley out.

It was not respect for age and position that stopped him. It was certainly not that Potterley's arguments had convinced him. Rather, it was a small point of college pride.

Why didn't M.I.T. give a course in neutrinics? For that

matter, now that he came to think of it, he doubted that there was a single book on neutrinics in the library. He could never recall having seen one.

He stopped to think about that.

And that was ruin.

Caroline Potterley had once been an attractive woman. There were occasions, such as dinners or university functions, when, by considerable effort, remnants of the attraction could be salvaged.

On ordinary occasions, she sagged. It was the word she applied to herself in moments of self-abhorrence. She had grown plumper with the years, but the flaccidity about her was not a matter of fat entirely. It was as though her muscles had given up and grown limp so that she shuffled when she walked while her eyes grew baggy and her cheeks jowly. Even her graying hair seemed tired rather than merely stringy. Its straightness seemed to be the result of a supine surrender to gravity, nothing else.

Caroline Potterley looked at herself in the mirror and admitted this was one of her bad days. She knew the reason, too.

It had been the dream of Laurel. The strange one, with Laurel grown up. She had been wretched ever since.

Still, she was sorry she had mentioned it to Arnold. He didn't say anything; he never did any more; but it was bad for him. He was particularly withdrawn for days afterward. It might have been that he was getting ready for that important conference with the big government official (he kept saying he expected no success), but it might also have been her dream.

It was better in the old days when he would cry sharply at her, 'Let the dead past *go*, Caroline! Talk won't bring her back, and dreams won't either.'

It had been bad for both of them. Horribly bad. She had been away from home and had lived in guilt ever since. If she had stayed at home, if she had not gone on an unnecessary shopping expedition, there would have been two of them available. One would have succeeded in saving Laurel.

Poor Arnold had not managed. Heaven knew he tried. He

43

had nearly died himself. He had come out of the burning house, staggering in agony, blistered, choking, half-blinded, with the dead Laurel in his arms.

The nightmare of that lived on, never lifting entirely.

Arnold slowly grew a shell about himself afterward. He cultivated a low-voiced mildness through which nothing broke, no lightning struck. He grew puritanical and even abandoned his minor vices, his cigarettes, his penchant for an occasional profane exclamation. He obtained his grant for the preparation of a new history of Carthage and subordinated everything to that.

She tried to help him. She hunted up his references, typed his notes and mircofilmed them. Then that ended suddenly.

She ran from the desk suddenly one evening, reaching the bathroom in bare time and retching abominably. Her husband followed her in confusion and concern.

'Caroline, what's wrong?'

It took a drop of brandy to bring her around. She said, 'Is it true? What they did?'

'Who did?'

'The Carthaginians.'

He stared at her and she got it out by indirection. She couldn't say it right out.

The Carthaginians, it seemed, worshiped Moloch, in the form of a hollow, brazen idol with a furnace in its belly. At times of national crisis, the priests and the people gathered, and infants, after the proper ceremonies and invocations, were dexterously hurled, alive, into the flames.

They were given sweetmeats just before the crucial moment, in order that the efficacy of the sacrifice not be ruined by displeasing cries of panic. The drums rolled just after the moment, to drown out the few seconds of infant shrieking. The parents were present, presumably gratified, for the sacrifice was pleasing to the gods. . . .

Arnold Potterley frowned darkly. Vicious lies, he told her, on the part of Carthage's enemies. He should have warned her. After all, such propagandistic lies were not uncommon. According to the Greeks, the ancient Hebrews worshiped an ass's head in their Holy of Holies. According to the Romans, the primitive Christians were haters of all men who sacrificed pagan children in the catacombs.

'Then they didn't do it?' asked Caroline.

'I'm sure they didn't. The primitive Phoenicians may have. Human sacrifice is commonplace in primitive cultures. But Carthage in her great days was not a primitive culture. Human sacrifice often gives way to symbolic actions such as circumcision. The Greeks and Romans might have mistaken some Carthaginian symbolism for the original full rite, either out of ignorance or out of malice.'

'Are you sure?'

'I can't be sure yet, Caroline, but when I've got enough evidence, I'll apply for permission to use chronoscopy, which will settle the matter once and for all.'

'Chronoscopy?'

'Time viewing. We can focus on ancient Carthage at some time of crisis, the landing of Scipio Africanus in 202 B.C., for instance, and see with our own eyes exactly what happens. And you'll see, I'll be right.'

He patted her and smiled encouragingly, but she dreamed of Laurel every night for two weeks thereafter and she never helped him with his Carthage project again. Nor did he ever ask her to.

But now she was bracing herself for his coming. He had called her after arriving back in town, told her he had seen the government man and that it had gone as expected. That meant failure, and yet the little telltale sign of depression had been absent from his voice and his features had appeared quite composed in the teleview. He had another errand to take care of, he said, before coming home.

It meant he would be late, but that didn't matter. Neither one of them was particular about eating hours or cared when packages were taken out of the freezer or even which packages or when the self-warming mechanism was activated.

When he did arrive, he surprised her. There was nothing untoward about him in any obvious way. He kissed her dutifully and smiled, took off his hat and asked if all had been well while he was gone. It was all almost perfectly normal. Almost.

She had learned to detect small things, though, and his

45

pace in all this was a trifle hurried. Enough to show her accustomed eye that he was under tension.

She said, 'Has something happened?'

He said, 'We're going to have a dinner guest night after next, Caroline. You don't mind?'

'Well, no. Is it anyone I know?'

'No. A young instructor. A newcomer. I've spoken to him.' He suddenly whirled toward her and seized her arms at the elbow, held them a moment, then dropped them in confusion as though disconcerted at having shown emotion.

He said, 'I almost didn't get through to him. Imagine that. Terrible, *terrible*, the way we have all bent to the yoke; the affection we have for the harness about us.'

Mrs. Potterley wasn't sure she understood, but for a year she had been watching him grow quietly more rebellious; little by little more daring in his criticism of the government. She said, 'You haven't spoken foolishly to him, have you?'

'What do you mean, foolishly? He'll be doing some neutrinics for me.'

'Neutrinics' was trisyllabic nonsense to Mrs. Potterley, but she knew it had nothing to do with history. She said faintly, 'Arnold, I don't like you to do that. You'll lose your position. It's —'

'It's intellectual anarchy, my dear,' he said. 'That's the phrase you want. Very well. I am an anarchist. If the government will not allow me to push my researches, I will push them on my own. And when I show the way, others will follow.... And if they don't, it makes no difference. It's Carthage that counts and human knowledge, not you and I.'

'But you don't know this young man. What if he is an agent for the Commissioner of Research.'

'Not likely and I'll take that chance.' He made a fist of his right hand and rubbed it gently against the palm of his left. 'He's on my side now. I'm sure of it. He can't help but be. I can recognize intellectual curiosity when I see it in a man's eyes and face and attitude, and it's a fatal disease for a tame scientist. Even today it takes time to beat it out of a man and the young ones are vulnerable.... Oh, why stop at anything? Why not build our own chronoscope and tell the

46

government to go to —'

He stopped abruptly, shook his head and turned away.

'I hope everything will be all right,' said Mrs. Potterley, feeling helplessly certain that everything would not be, and frightened, in advance, for her husband's professorial status and the security of their old age.

It was she alone, of them all, who had a violent presentiment of trouble. Quite the wrong trouble, of course.

Jonas Foster was nearly half an hour late in arriving at the Potterley's off-campus house. Up to that very evening, he had not quite decided he would go. Then, at the last moment, he found he could not bring himself to commit the social enormity of breaking a dinner appointment an hour before the appointed time. That, and the nagging of curiosity.

The dinner itself passed interminably. Foster ate without appetite. Mrs. Potterley sat in distant absent-mindedness, emerging out of it only once to ask if he were married and to make a deprecating sound at the news that he was not. Dr. Potterley himself asked neutrally after his professional history and nodded his head primly.

It was as staid, stodgy – boring, actually – as anything could be.

Foster thought: He seems so harmless.

Foster had spent the last two days reading up on Dr. Potterley. Very casually, of course, almost sneakily. He wasn't particularly anxious to be seen in the Social Science Library. To be sure, history was one of those borderline affairs and historical works were frequently read for amusement or edification by the general public.

Still, a physicist wasn't quite the 'general public'. Let Foster take to reading histories and he would be considered queer, sure as relativity, and after a while the Head of the Department would wonder if his new instructor were really 'the man for the job'.

So he had been cautious. He sat in the more secluded alcoves and kept his head bent when he slipped in and out at odd hours.

Dr. Potterley, it turned out, had written three books and

some dozen articles on the ancient Mediterranean worlds, and the later articles (all in 'Historical Reviews') had all dealt with pre-Roman Carthage from a sympathetic viewpoint.

That, at least, checked with Potterley's story and had soothed Foster's suspicions somewhat.... And yet Foster felt that it would have been much wiser, much safer, to have scotched the matter at the beginning.

A scientist shouldn't be too curious, he thought in bitter dissatisfaction with himself. It's a dangerous trait.

After dinner, he was ushered into Potterley's study and he was brought up sharply at the threshold. The walls were simply lined with books.

Not merely films. There were films, of course, but these were far outnumbered by the books – print on paper. He wouldn't have thought so many books would exist in usable condition.

That bothered Foster. Why should anyone want to keep so many books at home? Surely all were available in the university library, or, at the very worst, at the Library of Congress, if one wished to take the minor trouble of checking out a microfilm.

There was an element of secrecy involved in a home library. It breathed of intellectual anarchy. That last thought, oddly, calmed Foster. He would rather Potterley be an authentic anarchist than a play-acting *agent provocateur*.

And now the hours began to pass quickly and astonishingly.

'You see,' Potterley said, in a clear, unflurried voice, 'it was a matter of finding, if possible, anyone who had ever used chronoscopy in his work. Naturally, I couldn't ask baldly, since that would be unauthorized research.'

'Yes,' said Foster dryly. He was a little surprised such a small consideration would stop the man.

'I used indirect methods —'

He had. Foster was amazed at the volume of correspondence dealing with small disputed points of ancient Mediterranean culture which somehow managed to elicit the casual remark over and over again: 'Of course, having never made use of chronoscopy —' or, 'Pending approval of my request for chronoscopic data, which appears unlikely at the moment —'

'Now these aren't blind questionings,' said Potterley. 'There's a monthly booklet put out by the Institute for Chronoscopy in which items concerning the past as determined by time viewing are printed. Just one or two items.'

'What impressed me first was the triviality of most of the items, their insipidity. Why should such researches get priority over my work? So I wrote to people who would be most likely to do research in the directions described in the booklet. Uniformly, as I have shown you, they did *not* make use of the chronoscope. Now let's go over it point by point.'

At last Foster, his head swimming with Potterley's meticulously gathered details, asked, 'But why?'

'I don't know why,' said Potterley, 'but I have a theory. The original invention of the chronoscope was by Sterbinski – you see, I know that much – and it was well publicized. But then the government took over the instrument and decided to suppress further research in the matter or any use of the machine. But then, people might be curious as to why it wasn't being used. Curiosity is such a vice, Dr. Foster.'

Yes, agreed the physicist to himself.

'Imagine the effectiveness, then,' Potterley went on, 'of pretending that the chronoscope *was* being used. It would then be not a mystery, but a commonplace. It would no longer be a fitting object for legitimate curiosity or an attractive one for illicit curiosity.'

'*You* were curious,' pointed out Foster.

Potterley looked a trifle restless. 'It was different in my case,' he said angrily. 'I have something that *must* be done, and I wouldn't submit to the ridiculous way in which they kept putting me off.'

A bit paranoid, too, thought Foster gloomily.

Yet he had ended up with something, paranoid or not. Foster could no longer deny that something peculiar was going on in the matter of neutrinics.

But what was Potterley after? That still bothered Foster. If Potterley didn't intend this as a test of Foster's ethics, what *did* he want?

Foster put it to himself logically. If an intellectual anarchist with a touch of paranoia wanted to use a chronoscope and was convinced that the powers-that-be were deliberately standing in his way, what would he do?

Supposing it were I, he thought. What would I do?

He said slowly, 'Maybe the chronoscope doesn't exist at all?'

Potterley started. There was almost a crack in his general calmness. For an instant, Foster found himself catching a glimpse of something not at all calm.

But the historian kept his balance and said, 'Oh, no, there *must* be a chronoscope.'

'Why? Have you seen it? Have I? Maybe that's the explanation of everything. Maybe they're not deliberately holding out on a chronoscope they've got. Maybe they haven't got it in the first place.'

'But Sterbinski lived. He built a chronoscope. That much is a fact.'

'The book says so,' said Foster coldly.

'Now listen.' Potterley actually reached over and snatched at Foster's jacket sleeve. 'I need the chronoscope. I must have it. Don't tell me it doesn't exist. What we're going to do is find out enough about neutrinics to be able to —'

Potterley drew himself up short.

Foster drew his sleeve away. He needed no ending to that sentence. He supplied it himself. He said, 'Build one of our own?'

Potterley looked sour as though he would rather not have said it point-blank. Nevertheless, he said, 'Why not?'

'Because that's out of the question,' said Foster. 'If what I've read is correct, then it took Sterbinski twenty years to build his machine and several millions in composite grants. Do you think you and I can duplicate that illegally? Suppose we had the time, which we haven't, and suppose I could learn enough out of books, which I doubt, where would we get the money and equipment? The chronoscope is supposed to fill a five-story building, for Heaven's sake.'

'Then you won't help me?'

'Well, I'll tell you what. I have one way in which I may be able to find out something —'

'What is that?' asked Potterley at once.

'Never mind. That's not important. But I may be able to find out enough to tell you whether the government is deliberately suppressing research by chronoscope. I may confirm the evidence you already have or I may be able to prove that your evidence is misleading. I don't know what good it will do you in either case, but it's as far as I can go. It's my limit.'

Potterley watched the young man go finally. He was angry with himself. Why had he allowed himself to grow so careless as to permit the fellow to guess that he was thinking in terms of a chronoscope of his own. That was premature.

But then why did the young fool have to suppose that a chronoscope might not exist at all?

It *had* to exist. It *had* to. What was the use of saying it didn't?

And why couldn't a second one be built? Science had advanced in the fifty years since Sterbinski. All that was needed was knowledge.

Let the youngster gather knowledge. Let him think a small gathering would be his limit. Having taken the path to anarchy, there would be no limit. If the boy were not driven onward by something in himself, the first steps would be error enough to force the rest. Potterley was quite certain he would not hesitate to use blackmail.

Potterley waved a last good-bye and looked up. It was beginning to rain.

Certainly! Blackmail if necessary, but he would not be stopped.

Foster steered his car across the bleak outskirts of town and scarcely noticed the rain.

He *was* a fool, he told himself, but he couldn't leave things as they were. He had to know. He damned his streak of undisciplined curiosity, but he had to know.

But he would go no further than Uncle Ralph. He swore mightily to himself that it would stop there. In that way, there would be no evidence against him, no real evidence. Uncle Ralph would be discreet.

In a way, he was secretly ashamed of Uncle Ralph. He hadn't mentioned him to Potterley partly out of caution and partly because he did not wish to witness the lifted eyebrow, the inevitable half-smile. Professional science writers, however useful, were a little outside the pale, fit only for patronizing contempt. The fact that, as a class, they made more money than did research scientists only made matters worse, of course.

Still, there were times when a science writer in the family could be a convenience. Not being really educated, they did not have to specialize. Consequently, a good science writer knew practically everything ... And Uncle Ralph was one of the best.

Ralph Nimmo had no college degree and was rather proud of it. 'A degree,' he once said to Jonas Foster, when both were considerably younger, 'is a first step down a ruinous highway. You don't want to waste it so you go on to graduate work and doctoral research. You end up a thorough-going ignoramus on everything in the world except for one subdivisional sliver of nothing.

'On the other hand, if you guard your mind carefully and keep it blank of any clutter of information till maturity is reached, filling it only with intelligence and training it only in clear thinking, you then have a powerful instrument at your disposal and you can become a science writer.'

Nimmo received his first assignment at the age of twenty-five, after he had completed his apprenticeship and been out in the field for less than three months. It came in the shape of a clotted manuscript whose language would impart no glimmering of understanding to any reader, however qualified, without careful study and some inspired guesswork. Nimmo took it apart and put it together again (after five long and exasperating interviews with the authors, who were biophysicists), making the language taut and meaningful and smoothing the style to a pleasant gloss.

'Why not?' he would say tolerantly to his nephew, who countered his strictures on degrees by berating him with his readiness to hang on the fringes of science. 'The fringe is important. Your scientists can't write. Why should they be expected to? They aren't expected to be grand masters at chess or virtuosos at the violin, so why expect them to know how to put words together? Why not leave that for specialists, too?

'Good Lord, Jonas, read your literature of a hundred years ago. Discount the fact that the science is out of date and that some of the expressions are out of date. Just try to read it and make sense out of it. It's just jaw-cracking, amateurish. Pages are published uselessly; whole articles which are either non-comprehensible or both.'

'But you don't get recognition, Uncle Ralph,' protested young Foster, who was getting ready to start his college career and was rather starry-eyed about it. 'You could be a terrific researcher.'

'I get recognition,' said Nimmo. 'Don't think for a minute I don't. Sure, a biochemist or a strato-meteorologist won't give me the time of day, but they pay me well enough. Just find out what happens when some first-class chemist finds the Commission has cut his year's allowance for science writing. He'll fight harder for enough funds to afford me, or someone like me, than to get a recording ionograph.'

He grinned broadly and Foster grinned back. Actually, he was proud of his paunchy, round-faced, stub-fingered uncle, whose vanity made him brush his fringe of hair futilely over the desert of his pate and made him dress like an unmade haystack because such negligence was his trademark. Ashamed, but proud, too.

And now Foster entered his uncle's cluttered apartment in no mood at all for grinning. He was nine years older now and so was Uncle Ralph. For nine more years, papers in every branch of science had come to him for polishing and a little of each had crept into his capacious mind.

Nimmo was eating seedless grapes, popping them into his mouth one at a time. He tossed a bunch to Foster who caught them by a hair, then bent to retrieve individual grapes that had torn loose and fallen to the floor.

'Let them be. Don't bother,' said Nimmo carelessly. 'Someone comes in here to clean once a week. What's up? Having trouble with your grant application write-up?'

'I haven't really got into that yet.'

'You haven't? Get a move on, boy. Are you waiting for me to offer to do the final arrangement?'

'I couldn't afford you, Uncle.'

'Aw, come on. It's all in the family. Grant me all popular publication rights and no cash need change hands.'

Foster nodded. 'If you're serious, it's a deal.'

'It's a deal.'

It was a gamble, of course, but Foster knew enough of Nimmo's science writing to realize it could pay off. Some dramatic discovery of public interest on primitive man or on a new surgical technique, or on any branch of spationautics could mean a very cash-attracting article in any of the mass media of communication.

It was Nimmo, for instance, who had written up, for scientific consumption, the series of papers by Bryce and co-workers that elucidated the fine structure of two cancer viruses, for which job he asked the picayune payment of fifteen hundred dollars, provided popular publication rights were included. He then wrote up, exclusively, the same work in semidramatic form for use in trimensional video for a twenty-thousand-dollar advance plus rental royalties that were still coming in after five years.

Foster said bluntly, 'What do you know about neutrinics, Uncle?'

'Neutrinics?' Nimmo's small eyes looked surprised. 'Are you working in that? I thought it was pseudo-gravitic optics.'

'It is p.g.o. I just happen to be asking about neutrinics.'

'That's a devil of a thing to be doing. You're stepping out of line. You know that, don't you?'

'I don't expect you to call the Commission because I'm a little curious about things.'

'Maybe I should before you get into trouble. Curiosity is an occupational danger with scientists. I've watched it work. One of them will be moving quietly along on a problem, then curiosity leads him up a strange creek. Next thing you know they've done so little on their proper problem, they can't justify for a project renewal. I've seen more —'

'All I want to know,' said Foster patiently, 'is what's been passing through your hands lately on neutrinics.'

Nimmo leaned back, chewing at a grape thoughtfully. 'Nothing. Nothing ever. I don't recall ever getting a paper on neutrinics.'

'What!' Foster was openly astonished. 'Then who does get the work?'

'Now that you ask,' said Nimmo, 'I don't know. Don't recall anyone talking about it at the annual conventions. I don't think much work is being done there.'

'Why not?'

'Hey, there, don't bark. I'm not doing anything. My guess would be —'

Foster was exasperated. 'Don't you know?'

'Hmp. I'll tell you what I know about neutrinics. It concerns the applications of neutrino movements and the forces involved —'

'Sure. Sure. Just as electronics deals with the applications of electron movements and the forces involved, and pseudo-gravitics deals with the applications of artificial gravitational fields. I didn't come to you for that. Is that all you know?'

'And,' said Nimmo with equanimity, 'neutrinics is the basis of time viewing and that *is* all I know.'

Foster slouched back in his chair and massaged one lean cheek with great intensity. He felt angrily dissatisfied. Without formulating it explicitly in his own mind, he had felt sure, somehow, that Nimmo would come up with some late reports, bring up interesting facets of modern neutrinics, send him back to Potterley able to say that the elderly historian was mistaken, that his data was misleading, his deductions mistaken.

Then he could have returned to his proper work.

But now ...

He told himself angrily: So they're not doing much work in the field. Does that make it deliberate suppression? What if neutrinics is a sterile discipline? Maybe it is. I don't know. Potterley doesn't. Why waste the intellectual resources of humanity on nothing? Or the work might be secret for some legitimate reason. It might be ...

The trouble was, he had to know. He couldn't leave things as they were now. *He couldn't!*

He said, 'Is there a text on neutrinics, Uncle Ralph? I

mean a clear and simple one. An elementary one.'

Nimmo thought, his plump cheeks puffing out with a series of sighs. 'You ask the damnedest questions. The only one I ever heard of was Sterbinski and somebody. I've never seen it, but I viewed something about it once.... Sterbinski and LaMarr, that's it.'

'Is that the Sterbinski who invented the chronoscope?'

'I think so. Proves the book ought to be good.'

'Is there a recent edition? Sterbinski died thirty years ago.' Nimmo shrugged and said nothing.

'Can you find out?'

They sat in silence for a moment, while Nimmo shifted his bulk to the creaking tune of the chair he sat on. Then the science writer said, 'Are you going to tell me what this is all about?'

'I can't. Will you help me anyway, Uncle Ralph? Will you get me a copy of the text?'

'Well, you've taught me all I know on pseudo-gravitics. I should be grateful. Tell you what – I'll help you on one condition.'

'Which is?'

The older man was suddenly very grave. 'That you be careful, Jonas. You're obviously way out of line whatever you're doing. Don't blow up your career just because you're curious about something you haven't been assigned to and which is none of your business. Understand?'

Foster nodded, but he hardly heard. He was thinking furiously.

A full week later, Ralph Nimmo eased his rotund figure into Jonas Foster's on-campus two-room combination and said, in a hoarse whisper, 'I've got something.'

'What?' Foster was immediately eager.

'A copy of Sterbinski and LaMarr.' He produced it, or rather a corner of it, from his ample topcoat.

Foster almost automatically eyed doors and windows to make sure they were closed and shaded respectively, then held out his hand.

The film case was flaking with age, and when he cracked it the film was faded and growing brittle. He said sharply,

56

'Is this all?'

'Gratitude, my boy, gratitude!' Nimmo sat down with a grunt, and reached into a pocket for an apple.

'Oh, I'm grateful, but it's so old.'

'And lucky to get it at that. I tried to get a film from the Congressional Library. No go. The book was restricted.'

'Then how did you get this?'

'Stole it.' He was biting crunchingly around the core. 'New York Public.'

'What?'

'Simple enough. I had access to the stacks, naturally. So I stepped over a chained railing when no one was around, dug this up, and walked out with it. They're very trusting out there. Meanwhile, they won't miss it in years. . . . Only you'd better not let anyone see it on you, nephew.'

Foster stared at the film as though it were literally hot.

Nimmo discarded the core and reached for a second apple. 'Funny thing, now. There's nothing more recent in the whole field of neutrinics. Not a monograph, not a paper, not a progress note. Nothing since the chronoscope.'

'Uh-huh,' said Foster absently.

Foster worked evenings in the Potterley home. He could not trust his own on-campus rooms for the purpose. The evening work grew more real to him than his own grant applications. Sometimes he worried about it but then that stopped, too.

His work consisted, at first, simply in viewing and reviewing the text film. Later it consisted in thinking (sometimes while a section of the book ran itself off through the pocket projector, disregarded).

Sometimes Potterley would come down to watch, to sit with prim, eager eyes, as though he expected thought processes to solidify and become visible in all their convolutions. He interfered in only two ways. He did not allow Foster to smoke and sometimes he talked.

It wasn't conversation talk, never that. Rather it was a low-voiced monologue with which, it seemed, he scarcely expected to command attention. It was much more as though he were relieving a pressure within himself.

Carthage! Always Carthage!

Carthage, the New York of the ancient Mediterranean. Carthage, commercial empire and queen of the seas. Carthage, all that Syracuse and Alexandria pretended to be. Carthage, maligned by her enemies and inarticulate in her own defense.

She had been defeated once by Rome and then driven out of Sicily and Sardinia, but came back to more than recoup her losses by new dominions in Spain, and raised up Hannibal to give the Romans sixteen years of terror.

In the end, she lost again a second time, reconciled herself to fate and built again with broken tools a limping life in shrunken territory, succeeding so well that jealous Rome deliberately forced a third war. And then Carthage, with nothing but bare hands and tenacity, built weapons and forced Rome into a two-year war that ended only with complete destruction of the city, the inhabitants throwing themselves into their flaming houses rather than surrender.

'Could people fight so for a city and a way of life as bad as the ancient writers painted it? Hannibal was a better general than any Roman and his soldiers were absolutely faithful to him. Even his bitterest enemies praised him. There was a Carthaginian. It is fashionable to say that he was an atypical Carthaginian, better than the others, a diamond placed in garbage. But then why was he so faithful to Carthage, even to his death after years of exile? They talk of Moloch —'

Foster didn't always listen but sometimes he couldn't help himself and he shuddered and turned sick at the bloody tale of child sacrifice.

But Potterley went on earnestly, 'Just the same, it isn't true. It's a twenty-five-hundred-year-old canard started by the Greeks and Romans. They had their own slaves, their crucifixions and torture, their gladiatorial contests. They weren't holy. The Moloch story is what later ages would have called war propaganda, the big lie. I can prove it was a lie. I can prove it and, by Heaven, I will – I will —'

He would mumble that promise over and over again in his earnestness.

Mrs. Potterley visited him also, but less frequently, usually on Tuesdays and Thursdays when Dr. Potterley himself had an evening course to take care of and was not present.

She would sit quietly, scarcely talking, face slack and doughy, eyes blank, her whole attitude distant and withdrawn.

The first time, Foster tried, uneasily, to suggest that she leave.

She said tonelessly, 'Do I disturb you?'

'No, of course not,' lied Foster restlessly. 'It's just that – that —' He couldn't complete the sentence.

She nodded, as though accepting an invitation to stay. Then she opened a cloth bag she had brought with her and took out a quire of vitron sheets which she proceeded to weave together by rapid, delicate movements of a pair of slender, tetra-faceted depolarizers, whose battery-fed wires made her look as though she were holding a large spider.

One evening, she said softly, 'My daughter, Laurel, is your age.'

Foster started, as much at the sudden unexpected sound of speech as at the words. He said, 'I didn't know you had a daughter, Mrs. Potterley.'

'She died. Years ago.'

The vitron grew under the deft manipulations into the uneven shape of some garment Foster could not yet identify. There was nothing left for him to do but mutter inanely, 'I'm sorry.'

Mrs. Potterley sighed. 'I dream about her often.' She raised her blue, distant eyes to him.

Foster winced and looked away.

Another evening she asked, pulling at one of the vitron sheets to loosen its gentle clinging to her dress, 'What is time viewing anyway?'

That remark broke into a particularly involved chain of thought, and Foster said snappishly, 'Dr. Potterley can explain.'

'He's tried to. Oh, my, yes. But I think he's a little impatient with me. He calls it chronoscopy most of the time. Do you actually see things in the past, like the trimensionals? Or does it just make little dot patterns like the computer you use?'

Foster stared at his hand computer with distaste. It worked well enough, but every operation had to be manually controlled and the answers were obtained in code. Now if he could use the school computer ... Well, why dream, he felt conspicuous enough, as it was, carrying a hand computer under his arm every evening as he left his office.

He said, 'I've never seen the chronoscope myself, but I'm under the impression that you actually see pictures and hear sound.'

'You can hear people talk, too?'

'I think so.' Then, half in desperation, 'Look here, Mrs. Potterley, this must be awfully dull for you. I realize you don't like to leave a guest all to himself, but really, Mrs. Potterley, you mustn't feel compelled —'

'I don't feel compelled,' she said. 'I'm sitting here, waiting.'

'Waiting? For what?'

She said composedly, 'I listened to you that first evening. The time you first spoke to Arnold. I listened at the door.'

He said, 'You did?'

'I know I shouldn't have, but I was awfully worried about Arnold. I had a notion he was going to do something he oughtn't and I wanted to hear what. And then when I heard —' She paused, bending close over the vitron and peering at it.

'Heard what, Mrs. Potterley?'

'That you wouldn't build a chronoscope.'

'Well, of course not.'

'I thought maybe you might change your mind.'

Foster glared at her. 'Do you mean you're coming down here hoping I'll build a chronoscope, waiting for me to build one?'

'I hope you do, Dr. Foster. Oh, I hope you do.'

It was as though, all at once, a fuzzy veil had fallen off her face, leaving all her features clear and sharp, putting color into her cheeks, life into her eyes, the vibrations of something approaching excitement into her voice.

'Wouldn't it be wonderful,' she whispered, 'to have one?

People of the past could live again. Pharaohs and kings and – just people. I hope you build one, Dr. Foster. I really – hope —'

She choked, it seemed, on the intensity of her own words and let the vitron sheets slip off her lap. She rose and ran up the basement stairs, while Foster's eyes followed her awkwardly fleeing body with astonishment and distress.

It cut deeper into Foster's nights and left him sleepless and painfully stiff with thought. It was almost a mental indigestion.

His grant requests went limping in, finally, to Ralph Nimmo. He scarcely had any hope for them. He thought numbly: They won't be approved.

If they weren't, of course, it would create a scandal in the department and probably mean his appointment at the university would not be renewed, come the end of the academic year.

He scarcely worried. It was the neutrino, the neutrino, only the neutrino. Its trail curved and veered sharply and led him breathlessly along uncharted pathways that even Sterbinski and LaMarr did not follow.

He called Nimmo. 'Uncle Ralph, I need a few things. I'm calling from off the campus.'

Nimmo's face in the video plate was jovial, but his voice was sharp. He said, 'What you need is a course in communication. I'm having a hell of a time pulling your application into one intelligible piece. If that's what you're calling about —'

Foster shook his head impatiently. 'That's *not* what I'm calling about. I need these.' He scribbled quickly on a piece of paper and held it up before the receiver.

Nimmo yiped. 'Hey, how many tricks do you think I can wangle?'

'You can get them, Uncle. You know you can.'

Nimmo reread the list of items with silent motions of his plump lips and looked grave.

'What happens when you put those things together?' he asked. Foster shook his head. 'You'll have exclusive popular publication rights to whatever turns up, the way it's always been. But please don't ask any questions now.'

'I can't do miracles, you know.'

'Do this one. You've got to. You're a science writer, not a research man. You don't have to account for anything. You've got friends and connections. They can look the other way, can't they, to get a break from you next publication time?'

'Your faith, nephew, is touching. I'll try.'

Nimmo succeeded. The material and equipment were brought over late one evening in a private touring car. Nimmo and Foster lugged it in with the grunting of men unused to manual labour.

Potterley stood at the entrance of the basement after Nimmo had left. He asked softly, 'What's this for?'

Foster brushed the hair off his forehead and gently massaged a sprained wrist. He said, 'I want to conduct a few simple experiments.'

'Really?' The historian's eyes glittered with excitement.

Foster felt exploited. He felt as though he were being led along a dangerous highway by the pull of pinching fingers on his nose; as though he could see the ruin clearly that lay in wait at the end of the path, yet walked eagerly and determinedly. Worst of all, he felt the compelling grip on his nose to be his own.

It was Potterley who began it, Potterley who stood there now, gloating; but the compulsion was his own.

Foster said sourly, 'I'll be wanting privacy now, Potterley. I can't have you and your wife running down here and annoying me.'

He thought: If that offends him, let him kick me out. Let him put an end to this.

In his heart, though, he did not think being evicted would stop anything.

But it did not come to that. Potterley was showing no signs of offense. His mild gaze was unchanged. He said, 'Of course, Dr. Foster, of course. All the privacy you wish.'

Foster watched him go. He was left still marching along the highway, perversely glad of it and hating himself for being glad.

He took to sleeping over on a cot in Potterley's basement

62

and spending his weekends there entirely.

During that period, preliminary word came through that his grants (as doctored by Nimmo) had been approved. The Department Head brought the word and congratulated him.

Foster stared back distantly and mumbled, 'Good. I'm glad,' with so little conviction that the other frowned and turned away without another word.

Foster gave the matter no further thought. It was a minor point, worth no notice. He was planning something that really counted, a climactic test for that evening.

One evening, a second and third and then, haggard and half beside himself with excitement, he called in Potterley.

Potterley came down the stairs and looked about at the home-made gadgetry. He said, in his soft voice, 'The electric bills are quite high. I don't mind the expense, but the City may ask questions. Can anything be done?'

It was a warm evening, but Potterley wore a tight collar and a semi-jacket. Foster, who was in his undershirt, lifted bleary eyes and said shakily, 'It won't be for much longer, Dr. Potterley. I've called you down to tell you something. A chronoscope can be built. A small one, of course, but it can be built.'

Potterley seized the railing. His body sagged. He managed a whisper. 'Can it be built here?'

'Here in the basement,' said Foster wearily.

'Good Lord. You said —'

'I know what I said,' cried Foster impatiently. 'I said it couldn't be done. I didn't know anything then. Even Sterbinski didn't know anything.'

Potterley shook his head. 'Are you sure? You're not mistaken, Dr. Foster? I couldn't endure it if —'

Foster said, 'I'm not mistaken. Damn it, sir, if just theory had been enough, we could have had a time viewer over a hundred years ago, when the neutrino was first postulated. The trouble was, the original investigators considered it only a mysterious particle without mass or charge that could not be detected. It was just something to even up the bookkeeping and save the law of conservation of mass energy.'

He wasn't sure Potterley knew what he was talking about.

He didn't care. He needed a breather. He had to get some of this out of his clotting thoughts.... And he needed background for what he would have to tell Potterley next.

He went on. 'It was Sterbinski who first discovered that the neutrino broke through the space-time cross-sectional barrier, that it traveled through time as well as through space. It was Sterbinski who first devised a method for stopping neutrinos. He invented a neutrino recorder and learned how to interpret the pattern of the neutrino stream. Naturally, the stream had been affected and deflected by all the matter it had passed through in its passage through time, and the deflections could be analyzed and converted into the images of the matter that had done the deflecting. Time viewing was possible. Even air vibrations could be detected in this way and converted into sound.'

Potterley was definitely not listening. He said, 'Yes. Yes. But when can you build a chronoscope?'

Foster said urgently, 'Let me finish. Everything depends on the method used to detect and analyze the neutrino stream. Sterbinski's method was difficult and roundabout. It required mountains of energy. But I've studied pseudo-gravities, Dr. Potterley, the science of artificial gravitational fields. I've specialized in the behavior of light in such fields. It's a new science. Sterbinski knew nothing of it. If he had, he would have seen – anyone would have – a much better and more efficient method of detecting neutrinos using a pseudo-gravitic field. If I had known more neutrinics to begin with, I would have seen it at once.'

Potterley brightened a bit. 'I knew it,' he said. 'Even if they stop research in neutrinics there is no way the government can be sure that discoveries in other segments of science won't reflect knowledge on neutrinics. So much for the value of centralized direction of science. I thought this long ago, Dr. Foster, before you ever came to work here.'

'I congratulate you on that,' said Foster, 'but there's one thing —'

'Oh, never mind all this. Answer me. Please. When can you build a chronoscope?'

'I'm trying to tell you something, Dr. Potterley. A chronoscope won't do you any good.' (This is it, Foster thought.)

Slowly, Potterley descended the stairs. He stood facing Foster. 'What do you mean? Why won't it help me?'

'You won't see Carthage. It's what I've got to tell you. It's what I've been leading up to. You can never see Carthage.'

Potterley shook his head slightly. 'Oh no, you're wrong. If you have the chronoscope, just focus it properly —'

'No, Dr. Potterley. It's not a question of focus. There are random factors affecting the neutrino stream, as they affect all subatomic particles. What we call the uncertainty principle. When the stream is recorded and interpreted, the random factor comes out as fuzziness, or "noise" as the communication boys speak of it. The further back in time you penetrate, the more pronounced the fuzziness, the greater the noise. After a while, the noise drowns out the picture. Do you understand?'

'More power,' said Potterley in a dead kind of voice.

'That won't help. When the noise blurs out detail, magnifying detail magnifies the noise, too. You can't see anything in a sunburned film by enlarging it, can you? Get this through your head, now. The physical nature of the universe sets limits. The random thermal motions of air molecules set limits to how weak a sound can be detected by any instrument. The length of a light wave or of an electron wave sets limits to the size of objects that can be seen by any instrument. It works that way in chronoscopy, too. You can only time view so far.'

'How far? How far?'

Foster took a deep breath. 'A century and a quarter. That's the most.'

'But the monthly bulletin the Commission puts out deals with ancient history almost entirely.' The historian laughed shakily. 'You must be wrong. The government has data as far back as 3000 B.C.'

'When did you switch to believing them?' demanded Foster, scornfully. 'You began this business by proving they were lying; that no historian had made use of the chronoscope. Don't you see why now? No historian, except one interested in contemporary history, could. No chronoscope can possibly see back in time further than 1920 under any conditions.'

65

'You're wrong. You don't know everything,' said Potterley.

'The truth won't bend itself to your convenience either. Face it. The government's part in this is to perpetuate a hoax.'

'Why?'

'I don't know why.'

Potterley's snubby nose was twitching. His eyes were bulging. He pleaded, 'It's only theory, Dr. Foster. Build a chronoscope. Build one and try.'

Foster caught Potterley's shoulders in a sudden, fierce grip. 'Do you think I haven't? Do you think I would tell you this before I had checked it every way I knew? I *have* built one. It's all around you. Look!'

He ran to the switches at the power leads. He flicked them on, one by one. He turned a resistor, adjusted other knobs, put out the cellar lights. 'Wait. Let it warm up.'

There was a small glow near the centre of one wall. Potterley was gibbering incoherently, but Foster only cried again, 'Look!'

The light sharpened and brightened, broke up into a light-and-dark pattern. Men and women! Fuzzy. Features blurred. Arms and legs mere streaks. An old-fashioned ground car, unclear but recognizable as one of the kind that had once used gasoline-powered internal-combustion engines, sped by.

Foster said, 'Mid-twentieth century, somewhere. I can't hook up an audio yet so this is soundless. Eventually, we can add sound. Anyway, mid-twentieth is almost as far back as you can go. Believe me, that's the best focusing that can be done.'

Potterley said, 'Build a larger machine, a stronger one. Improve your circuits.'

'You can't lick the Uncertainty Principle, man, any more than you can live on the sun. There are physical limits to what can be done.'

'You're lying. I won't believe you. I —'

A new voice sounded, raised shrilly to make itself heard.

'Arnold! Dr. Foster!'

The young physicist turned at once. Dr. Potterley froze

for a long moment, then said, without turning, 'What is it, Caroline? Leave us.'

'No!' Mrs. Potterley descended the stairs. 'I heard. I couldn't help hearing. Do you have a time viewer here, Dr. Foster? Here in the basement?'

'Yes, I do, Mrs. Potterley. A kind of time viewer. Not a good one. I can't get sound yet and the picture is darned blurry, but it works.'

Mrs. Potterley clasped her hands and held them tightly against her breast. 'How wonderful. How wonderful.'

'It's not at all wonderful,' snapped Potterley. 'The young fool can't reach further back than —'

'Now, look,' began Foster in exasperation. . . .

'Please!' cried Mrs. Potterley. 'Listen to me. Arnold, don't you see that as long as we can use it for twenty years back, we can see Laurel once again? What do we care about Carthage and ancient times? It's Laurel we can see. She'll be alive for us again. Leave the machine here, Dr. Foster. Show us how to work it.'

Foster stared at her, then at her husband. Dr. Potterley's face had gone white. Though his voice stayed low and even, its calmness was somehow gone. He said, 'You're a fool!'

Caroline said weakly, 'Arnold!'

'You're a fool, I say. What will you see? The past. The dead past. Will Laurel do one thing she did not do? Will you see one thing you haven't seen? Will you live three years over and over again, watching a baby who'll never grow up no matter how you watch?'

His voice came near to cracking, but held. He stepped closer to her, seized her shoulder and shook her roughly. 'Do you know what will happen to you if you do that? They'll come to take you away because you'll go mad. Yes, mad. Do you want mental treatment? Do you want to be shut up, to undergo the psychic probe?'

Mrs. Potterley tore away. There was no trace of softness or vagueness about her. She had twisted into a virago. 'I want to see my child, Arnold. She's in that machine and I want her.'

'She's not in the machine. An image is. Can't you understand? An image! Something that's not real!'

'I want my child. Do you hear me?' She flew at him, screaming, fists beating. *I want my child.*

The historian retreated at the fury of the assault, crying out. Foster moved to step between, when Mrs. Potterley dropped, sobbing wildly, to the floor.

Potterley turned, eyes desperately seeking. With a sudden heave, he snatched at a Lando-rod, tearing it from its support, and whirling away before Foster, numbed by all that was taking place, could move to stop him.

'Stand back!' gasped Potterley, 'or I'll kill you. I swear it.' He swung with force, and Foster jumped back.

Potterley turned with fury on every part of the structure in the cellar, and Foster, after the first crash of glass, watched dazedly.

Potterley spent his rage and then he was standing quietly amid shards and splinters, with a broken Lando-rod in his hand. He said to Foster in a whisper, 'Now get out of here! Never come back! If any of this cost you anything, send me a bill and I'll pay for it. I'll pay double.'

Foster shrugged, picked up his shirt and moved up the basement stairs. He could hear Mrs. Potterley sobbing loudly, and, as he turned at the head of the stairs for a last look, he saw Dr. Potterley bending over her, his face convulsed with sorrow.

Two days later, with the school day drawing to a close, and Foster looking wearily about to see if there were any data on his newly approved projects that he wished to take home, Dr. Potterley appeared once more. He was standing at the open door of Foster's office.

The historian was neatly dressed as ever. He lifted his hand in a gesture that was too vague to be a greeting, too abortive to be a plea. Foster stared stonily.

Potterley said, 'I waited till five, till you were ... May I come in?'

Foster nodded.

Potterley said, 'I suppose I ought to apologize for my behavior. I was dreadfully disappointed, not quite master of myself. Still, it was inexcusable.'

'I accept your apology,' said Foster. 'Is that all?'

'My wife called you, I think?'

'Yes, she has.'

'She has been quite hysterical. She told me she had but I couldn't be quite sure —'

'She has called me.'

'Could you tell me – would you be so kind as to tell me what she wanted?'

'She wanted a chronoscope. She said she had some money of her own. She was willing to pay.'

'Did you – make any commitments?'

'I said I wasn't in the manufacturing business.'

'Good,' breathed Potterley, his chest expanding with a sigh of relief. 'Please don't take any calls from her. She's not – quite —'

'Look, Dr. Potterley,' said Foster, 'I'm not getting into any domestic quarrels, but you'd better be prepared for something. Chronoscopes can be built by anybody. Given a few simple parts that can be bought through some etherics sales centre, it can be built in the home workshop. The video part, anyway.'

'But no one else will think of it beside you, will they? No one has.'

'I don't intend to keep it secret.'

'But you can't publish. It's illegal research.'

'That doesn't matter any more, Dr. Potterley. If I lose my grants, I lose them. If the university is displeased, I'll resign. It just doesn't matter.'

'But you can't do that!'

'Till now,' said Foster, 'you didn't mind my risking loss of grants and position. Why do you turn so tender about it now? Now let me explain something to you. When you first came to me, I believed in organized and directed research; the situation as it existed, in other words. I considered you an intellectual anarchist, Dr. Potterley, and dangerous. But, for one reason or another, I've been an anarchist myself for months now and I have achieved great things.

'Those things have been achieved not because I am a brilliant scientist. Not at all. It was just that scientific research had been directed from above and holes were left that could be filled in by anyone who looked in the right direction. And anyone might have if the government hadn't actively tried to prevent it.

'Now understand me. I still believe directed research can be useful. I'm not in favor of a retreat to total anarchy. But there must be a middle ground. Directed research can retain flexibility. A scientist must be allowed to follow his curiosity, at least in his spare time.'

Potterley sat down. He said ingratiatingly, 'Let's discuss this, Foster. I appreciate your idealism. You're young. You want the moon. But you can't destroy yourself through fancy notions of what research must consist of. I got you into this. I am responsible and I blame myself bitterly. I was acting emotionally. My interest in Carthage blinded me and I was a damn fool.'

Foster broke in. 'You mean you've changed completely in two days? Carthage is nothing? Government suppression of research is nothing?'

'Even a damn fool like myself can learn, Foster. My wife taught me something. I understand the reason for government suppression of neutrinics now. I didn't two days ago. And, understanding, I approve. You saw the way my wife reacted to the news of a chronoscope in the basement. I had envisioned a chronoscope used for research purposes. All *she* could see was the personal pleasure of returning neurotically to a personal past, a dead past. The pure researcher, Foster, is in the minority. People like my wife would outweigh us.

'For the government to encourage chronoscopy would have meant that everyone's past would be visible. The government officers would be subjected to blackmail and improper pressure, since who on Earth has a past that is absolutely clean? Organized government might become impossible.'

Foster licked his lips. 'Maybe. Maybe the government has some justification in its own eyes. Still, there's an important principle involved here. Who knows what other scientific advances are being stymied because scientists are being stifled into walking a narrow path? If the chronoscope becomes the terror of a few politicians, it's a price that must be paid. The public must realize that science must be free and there is no more dramatic way of doing it than to publish my discovery, one way or another, legally or illegally.'

Potterley's brow was damp with perspiration, but his voice remained even. 'Oh, not just a few politicians, Dr. Foster. Don't think that. It would be my terror, too. My wife would spend her time living with our dead daughter. She would retreat further from reality. She would go mad living the same scenes over and over. And not just my terror. There would be others like her. Children searching for their dead parents or their own youth. We'll have a whole world living in the past. Midsummer madness.'

Foster said, 'Moral judgments can't stand in the way. There isn't one advance at any time in history that mankind hasn't had the ingenuity to prevent. Mankind must also have the ingenuity to prevent. As for the chronoscope, your delvers into the dead past will get tired soon enough. They'll catch their loved parents in some of the things their loved parents did and they'll lose their enthusiasm for it all. But all this is trivial. With me, it's a matter of important principle.'

Potterley said, 'Hang your principle. Can't you understand men and women as well as principle? Don't you understand that my wife will live through the fire that killed our baby? She won't be able to help herself. I know her. She'll follow through each step, trying to prevent it. She'll live it over and over again, hoping each time that it won't happen. How many times do you want to kill Laurel?' A huskiness had crept into his voice.

A thought crossed Foster's mind. 'What are you really afraid she'll find out, Dr. Potterley? What happened the night of the fire?'

The historian's hands went up quickly to cover his face and they shook with his dry sobs. Foster turned away and stared uncomfortably out of the window.

Potterley said after a while, 'It's a long time since I've had to think of it. Caroline was away. I was baby-sitting. I went into the baby's bedroom midevening to see if she had kicked off the bedclothes. I had my cigarette with me ... I smoked in those days. I must have stubbed it out before putting it in the ashtray on the chest of drawers. I was always careful.

71

The baby was all right. I returned to the living room and fell asleep before the video. I awoke, choking, surrounded by fire. I don't know how it started.'

'But you think it may have been the cigarette, is that it?' said Foster. 'A cigarette which, for once, you forgot to stub out?'

'I don't know. I tried to save her, but she was dead in my arms when I got out.'

'You never told your wife about the cigarette, I suppose.'

Potterley shook his head. 'But I've lived with it.'

'Only now, with a chronoscope, she'll find out. Maybe it wasn't the cigarette. Maybe you did stub it out. Isn't that possible?'

The scant tears had dried on Potterley's face. The redness had subsided. He said, 'I can't take the chance.... But it's not just myself, Foster. The past has its terrors for most people. Don't loose those terrors on the human race.'

Foster paced the floor. Somehow, this explained the reason for Potterley's rabid, irrational desire to boost the Carthaginians, deify them, most of all disprove the story of their fiery sacrifices to Moloch. By freeing them of the guilt of infanticide by fire, he symbolically freed himself of the same guilt.

So the same fire that had driven him on to causing the construction of a chronoscope was now driving him on to its destruction.

Foster looked sadly at the older man. 'I see your position, Dr. Potterley, but this goes above personal feelings. I've got to smash this throttling hold on the throat of science.'

Potterley said, savagely, 'You mean you want the fame and wealth that goes with such a discovery.'

'I don't know about the wealth, but that, too, I suppose. I'm no more than human.'

'You won't suppress your knowledge?'

'Not under any circumstances.'

'Well, then —' and the historian got to his feet and stood for a moment, glaring.

Foster had an odd moment of terror. The man was older than he, smaller, feebler, and he didn't look armed. Still . . .

Foster said, 'If you're thinking of killing me or anything

72

insane like that, I've got the information in a safety-deposit vault where the proper people will find it in case of my disappearance or death.'

Potterley said, 'Don't be a fool,' and stalked out.

Foster closed the door, locked it and sat down to think. He felt silly. He had no information in any safety-deposit vault, of course. Such a melodramatic action would not have occurred to him ordinarily. But now it had.

Feeling even sillier, he spent an hour writing out the equations of the application of pseudo-gravitic optics to neutrinic recording, and some diagrams for the engineering details of construction. He sealed it in an envelope and scrawled Ralph Nimmo's name over the outside.

He spent a rather restless night and the next morning, on the way to school, dropped the envelope off at the bank, with appropriate instructions to an official, who made him sign a paper permitting the box to be opened after his death.

He called Nimmo to tell him of the existence of the envelope, refusing querulously to say anything about its contents.

He had never felt so ridiculously self-conscious as at that moment.

That night and the next, Foster spent in only fitful sleep, finding himself face to face with the highly practical problem of the publication of data unethically obtained.

The *Proceedings of the Society for Pseudo-Gravitics*, which was the journal with which he was best acquainted, would certainly not touch any paper that did not include the magic footnote: 'The work described in this paper was made possible by Grant No. so-and-so from the Commission of Research of the United Nations.'

Nor, doubly so, would the *Journal of Physics*.

There were always the minor journals who might overlook the nature of the article for the sake of the sensation, but that would require a little financial negotiation on which he hesitated to embark. It might, on the whole, be better to pay the cost of publishing a small pamphlet for general distribution among scholars. In that case, he would even be able to dispense with the services of a science writer, sacrificing polish for speed. He would have to find a reliable printer. Uncle Ralph might know one.

He walked down the corridor to his office and wondered anxiously if perhaps he ought to waste no further time, give himself no further chance to lapse into indecision and take the risk of calling Ralph from his office phone. He was so absorbed in his own heavy thoughts that he did not notice that his room was occupied until he turned from the clothes closet and approached his desk.

Dr. Potterley was there and a man whom Foster did not recognize.

Foster stared at them. 'What's this?'

Potterley said, 'I'm sorry, but I had to stop you.'

Foster continued staring. 'What are you talking about?'

The stranger said, 'Let me introduce myself.' He had large teeth, a little uneven, and they showed prominently when he smiled. 'I am Thaddeus Araman, Department Head of the Division of Chronoscopy. I am here to see you concerning information brought to me by Professor Arnold Potterley and confirmed by our own sources —'

Potterley said breathlessly, 'I took all the blame, Dr. Foster. I explained that it was I who persuaded you against your will into unethical practices. I have offered to accept full responsibility and punishment. I don't wish you harmed in any way. It's just that chronoscopy must not be permitted!'

Araman nodded. 'He has taken the blame as he says, Dr. Foster, but this thing is out of his hands now.'

Foster said, 'So? What are you going to do? Blackball me from all consideration for research grants?'

'That is in my power,' said Araman.

'Order the university to discharge me?'

'That, too, is in my power.'

'All right, go ahead. Consider it done. I'll leave my office now, with you. I can send for my books later. If you insist, I'll leave my books. Is that all?'

'Not quite,' said Araman. 'You must engage to do no further research in chronoscopy, to publish none of your findings in chronoscopy and, of course, to build no chronoscope. You will remain under surveillance indefinitely to

74

make sure you keep that promise.'

'Supposing I refuse to promise? What can you do? Doing research out of my field may be unethical, but it isn't a criminal offense.'

'In the case of chronoscopy, my young friend,' said Araman patiently, 'it is a criminal offense. If necessary, you will be put in jail and kept there.'

'Why?' shouted Foster. 'What's magic about chronoscopy?'

Araman said, 'That's the way it is. We cannot allow further developments in the field. My own job is, primarily, to make sure of that, and I intend to do my job. Unfortunately, I had no knowledge, nor did anyone in the department, that the optics of pseudo-gravity fields had such immediate application to chronoscopy. Score one for general ignorance, but henceforward research will be steered properly in that respect, too.'

Foster said, 'That won't help. Something else may apply that neither you nor I dream of. All science hangs together. It's one piece. If you want to stop one part, you've got to stop it all.'

'No doubt that is true,' said Araman, 'in theory. On the practical side, however, we have managed quite well to hold chronoscopy down to the original Sterbinski level for fifty years. Having caught you in time, Dr. Foster, we hope to continue doing so indefinitely. And we wouldn't have come this close to disaster, either, if I had accepted Dr. Potterley at something more than face value.'

He turned toward the historian and lifted his eyebrows in a kind of humorous self-deprecation. 'I'm afraid, sir, that I dismissed you as a history professor and no more on the occasion of our first interview. Had I done my job properly and checked on you, this would not have happened.'

Foster said abruptly, 'Is anyone allowed to use the government chronoscope?'

'No one outside our division under any pretext. I say that since it is obvious to me that you have already guessed as much. I warn you, though, that any repetition of that fact will be a criminal, not an ethical, offense.'

'And your chronoscope doesn't go back more than a

hundred and twenty-five years or so, does it?'

'It doesn't.'

'Then your bulletin with its stories of time viewing ancient times is a hoax?'

Araman said coolly, 'With the knowledge you now have, it is obvious you know that for a certainty. However, I confirm your remark. The monthly bulletin is a hoax.'

'In that case,' said Foster, 'I will not promise to suppress my knowledge of chronoscopy. If you wish to arrest me, go ahead. My defense at the trial will be enough to destroy the vicious card house of directed research and bring it tumbling down. Directing research is one thing; suppressing it and depriving mankind of its benefits is quite another.'

Araman said, 'Oh, let's get something straight, Dr. Foster. If you do not cooperate, you will go to jail directly. You will *not* see a lawyer, you will *not* be charged, you will *not* have a trial. You will simply stay in jail.'

'Oh no,' said Foster, 'you're bluffing. This is not the twentieth century, you know.'

There was a stir outside the office, the clatter of feet, a high-pitched shout that Foster was sure he recognized. The door crashed open, the lock splintering, and three intertwined figures stumbled in.

As they did so, one of the men raised a blaster and brought its butt down hard on the skull of another.

There was a whoosh of expiring air, and the one whose head was struck went limp.

'Uncle Ralph!' cried Foster.

Araman frowned. 'Put him down in that chair,' he ordered, 'and get some water.'

Ralph Nimmo, rubbing his head with a gingerly sort of disgust, said, 'There was no need to get rough, Araman.'

Araman said, 'The guard should have been rough sooner and kept you out of here, Nimmo. You'd have been better off.'

'You know each other?' asked Foster.

'I've had dealings with the man,' said Nimmo, still rubbing. 'If he's here in your office, nephew, you're in trouble.'

'And you, too,' said Araman angrily. 'I know Dr. Foster consulted you on neutrinics literature.'

Nimmo corrugated his forehead, then straightened it with a wince as though the action had brought pain. 'So?' he said. 'What else do you know about me?'

'We will know everything about you soon enough. Meanwhile, that one item is enough to implicate you. What are you doing here?'

'My dear Dr. Araman,' said Nimmo, some of his jauntiness restored, 'day before yesterday, my jackass of a nephew called me. He had placed some mysterious information —'

'Don't tell him! Don't say anything!' cried Foster.

Araman glanced at him coldly. 'We know all about it, Dr. Foster. The safety-deposit box has been opened and its contents removed.'

'But how can you know —' Foster's voice died away in a kind of furious frustration.

'Anyway,' said Nimmo, 'I decided the net must be closing around him and, after I took care of a few items, I came down to tell him to get off this thing he's doing. It's not worth his career.'

'Does that mean you know what he's doing?' asked Araman.

'He never told me,' said Nimmo, 'but I'm a science writer with a hell of a lot of experience. I know which side of an atom is electronified. The boy, Foster, specializes in pseudo-gravitic optics and coached me on the stuff himself. He got me to get him a textbook on neutrinics and I kind of skip-viewed it myself before handing it over. I can put the two together. He asked me to get him certain pieces of physical equipment, and that was evidence, too. Stop me if I'm wrong, but my nephew has built a semi-portable, low-power chronoscope. Yes, or – yes?'

'Yes.' Araman reached thoughtfully for a cigarette and paid no attention to Dr. Potterley (watching silently, as though all were a dream) who shied away, gasping, from the white cylinder. 'Another mistake for me. I ought to resign. I should have put tabs on you, too, Nimmo, instead of concentrating too hard on Potterley and Foster. I didn't have much time of course and you've ended up safely here, but that doesn't excuse me. You're under arrest, Nimmo.'

'What for?' demanded the science writer.

'Unauthorized research.'

'I wasn't doing any. I can't, not being a registered scientist. And even if I did, it's not a criminal offense.'

Foster said savagely, 'No use, Uncle Ralph. This bureaucrat is making his own laws.'

'Like what?' demanded Nimmo.

'Like life imprisonment without trial.'

'Nuts,' said Nimmo. 'This isn't the twentieth cen —'

'I tried that,' said Foster. 'It doesn't bother him.'

'Well, nuts,' shouted Nimmo. 'Look here, Araman. My nephew and I have relatives who haven't lost touch with us, you know. The professor has some also, I imagine. You can't just make us disappear. There'll be questions and a scandal. This *isn't* the twentieth century. So if you're trying to scare us, it isn't working.'

The cigarette snapped between Araman's fingers and he tossed it away violently. He said, 'Damn it, I don't know *what* to do. It's never been like this before.... Look! You three fools know nothing of what you're trying to do. You understand nothing. Will you listen to me?'

'Oh, we'll listen,' said Nimmo grimly.

(Foster sat silently, eyes angry, lips compressed. Potterley's hands writhed like two intertwined snakes.)

Araman said, 'The past to you is the dead past. If any of you have discussed the matter, it's dollars to nickels you've used that phrase. The dead past. If you knew how many times I've heard these three words, you'd choke on them, too.'

'When people think of the past, they think of it as dead, far away and gone, long ago. We encourage them to think so. When we report time viewing, we always talk of views centuries in the past, even though you gentlemen know seeing more than a century or so is impossible. People accept it. The past means Greece, Rome, Carthage, Egypt, the Stone Age. The deader the better.

'Now you three know a century or a little more is the limit, so what does the past mean to you? Your youth. Your first girl. Your dead mother. Twenty years ago. Thirty years ago. Fifty years ago. The deader the better.... But when does the past really begin?'

He paused in anger. The others stared at him and Nimmo stirred uneasily.

'Well,' said Araman, 'when did it begin? A year ago? Five minutes ago? One second ago? Isn't it obvious that the past begins an instant ago? The dead past is just another name for the living present. What if you focus the chronoscope in the past of one-hundredth of a second ago? Aren't you watching the present? Does it begin to sink in?'

Nimmo said, 'Damnation.'

'Damnation,' mimicked Araman. 'After Potterley came to me with his story night before last, how do you suppose I checked up on both of you? I did it with the chronoscope, spotting key moments to the very instant of the present.'

'And that's how you knew about the safety-deposit box?' said Foster.

'And every other important fact. Now what do you suppose would happen if we let news of a home chronoscope get out? People might start out by watching their youth, their parents and so on, but it wouldn't be long before they'd catch on to the possibilities. The housewife will forget her poor, dead mother and take to watching her neighbor at home and her husband at the office. The businessman will watch his competitor, the employer his employee.

'There will be no such thing as privacy. The party line, the prying eye behind the curtain will be nothing compared to it. The video stars will be closely watched at all times by everyone. Every man his own peeping Tom and there'll be no getting away from the watcher. Even darkness will be no escape because chronoscopy can be adjusted to the infrared and human figures can be seen by their own body heat. The figures will be fuzzy, of course, and the surroundings will be dark, but that will make the titillation of it all the greater, perhaps.... Hmp, the men in charge of the machine now experiment sometimes in spite of the regulations against it.'

Nimmo seemed sick. 'You can always forbid private manufacture —'

Araman turned on him fiercely. 'You can, but do you expect it to do any good? Can you legislate successfully against drinking, smoking, adultery or gossiping over the

79

back fence? And this mixture of nosiness and prurience will have a worse grip on humanity than any of those. Good Lord, in a thousand years of trying we haven't even been able to wipe out the heroin traffic and you talk about legislating against a device for watching anyone you please at any time you please that can be built in a home workshop.'

Foster said suddenly, 'I won't publish.'

Potterley burst out, half in sobs, 'None of us will talk. I regret —'

Nimmo broke in. 'You said you didn't tab me on the chronoscope, Araman.'

'No time,' said Araman wearily. 'Things don't move any faster on the chronoscope than in real life. You can't speed it up like the film in a book viewer. We spent a full twenty-four hours trying to catch the important moments during the last six months of Potterley and Foster. There was no time for anything else and it was enough.'

'It wasn't,' said Nimmo.

'What are you talking about?' There was a sudden infinite alarm on Araman's face.

'I told you my nephew, Jonas, had called me to say he had put important information in a safety-deposit box. He acted as though he were in trouble. He's my nephew. I had to try to get him off the spot. It took a while, then I came here to tell him what I had done. I told you when I got here, just after your man conked me, that I had taken care of a few items.'

'What? For Heaven's sake —'

'Just this: I sent the details of the portable chronoscope off to half a dozen of my regular publicity outlets.'

Not a word. Not a sound. Not a breath. They were all past any demonstration.

'Don't stare like that,' cried Nimmo. 'Don't you see my point? I had popular publication rights. Jonas will admit that. I knew he couldn't publish scientifically in any legal way. I was sure he was planning to publish illegally and was preparing the safety-deposit box for that reason. I thought if I put through the details prematurely, all the responsibility would be mine. His career would be saved. And if I were deprived of my science-writing licence as a result, my exclusive possession of the chronometric data would set me up for life. Jonas would be angry, I expected that, but I could explain the motive and we would split the take fifty-fifty.... Don't stare at me like that. How did I know —'

'Nobody knew anything,' said Araman bitterly, 'but you all just took it for granted that the government was stupidly bureaucratic, vicious, tyrannical, given to suppressing research for the hell of it. It never occurred to any of you that we were trying to protect mankind as best we could.'

'Don't sit there talking,' wailed Potterley. 'Get the names of the people who were told —'

'Too late,' said Nimmo, shrugging. 'They've had better than a day. There's been time for the word to spread. My outfits will have called any number of physicists to check my data before going on with it and they'll call one another to pass on the news. Once scientists put neutrinics and pseudo-gravitics together, home chronoscopy becomes obvious. Before the week is out, five hundred people will know how to build a small chronoscope and how will you catch them all?' His plump cheeks sagged. 'I suppose there's no way of putting the mushroom cloud back into that nice, shiny uranium sphere.'

Araman stood up. 'We'll try, Potterley, but I agree with Nimmo. It's too late. What kind of a world we'll have from now on, I don't know, I can't tell, but the world we know has been destroyed completely. Until now, every custom, every habit, every tiniest way of life has always taken a certain amount of privacy for granted, but that's all gone now.'

He saluted each of the three with elaborate formality.

'You have created a new world among the three of you. I congratulate you. Happy goldfish bowl to you, to me, to everyone, and may each of you fry in hell forever. Arrest rescinded.'

THE DYING NIGHT

It was almost a class reunion, and though it was marked by joylessness, there was no reason as yet to think it would be marred by tragedy.

Edward Talliaferro, fresh from the Moon and without his gravity legs yet, met the other two in Stanley Kaunas' room. Kaunas rose to greet him in a subdued manner. Battersley Ryger merely sat and nodded.

Talliaferro lowered his large body carefully to the couch, very aware of its unaccustomed weight. He grimaced a little, his plump lips twisting inside the rim of hair that surrounded them on lip, chin, and cheek.

They had seen one another earlier that day under more formal conditions. Now for the first time they were alone and Talliaferro said, 'This is a kind of occasion. We're meeting for the first time in ten years. First time since graduation, in fact.'

Ryger's nose twitched. It had been broken shortly before that same graduation and he had received his degree in astronomy with a bandage disfiguring his face. He said grumpily, 'Anyone ordered champagne? Or something?'

Talliaferro said, 'Come on! First big interplanetary astronomical convention in history is no place for glooming. And among friends, too!'

Kaunas said suddenly, 'It's Earth. It doesn't feel right. I can't get used to it.' He shook his head but his look of depression remained.

Talliaferro said, 'I know. I'm so heavy. It takes all the energy out of me. At that, you're better off than I am, Kaunas. Mercurian gravity is 0·4 normal. On the Moon, it's only 0·16.' He interrupted Ryger's beginning of a sound by saying, 'And on Ceres they use pseudo-grav fields adjusted to 0·8. You have no problems at all, Ryger.'

The Cerian astronomer looked annoyed. 'It's the open air. Going outside without a suit gets me.'

'Right,' agreed Kaunas. 'And letting the Sun beat down on you. Just letting it.'

Talliaferro found himself insensibly drifting back in time. They had not changed much. Nor, he thought, had he himself. They were all ten years older, of course. Ryger had put on some weight and Kaunas' thin face had grown a bit leathery, but he would have recognized either if he had met him without warning.

He said, 'I don't think it's Earth getting us. Let's face it.'

Kaunas looked up sharply. He was a little fellow with quick, nervous movements of his hands and habitually wore clothes that looked a shade too large for him.

He said, 'Villiers! I know, I think about him sometimes.' Then, with an air of desperation, 'I got a letter from him.'

Ryger sat upright, his olive complexion darkening further, and said with energy. 'You did? When?'

'A month ago.'

Ryger turned to Talliaferro. 'How about you?'

Talliaferro blinked placidly and nodded.

Ryger said, 'He's gone crazy. He claims he's discovered a practical method of mass transference through space. – He told you two also? – That's it, then. He was always a little bent. Now he's broken.'

He rubbed his nose fiercely and Talliaferro thought of the day Villiers had broken it.

For ten years Villiers had haunted them like the vague shadow of a guilt that wasn't really theirs. They had gone through their graduate work together, four picked and dedicated men being trained for a profession that had reached new heights in this age of interplanetary travel.

The observatories were opening on the other worlds, surrounded by vacuum, unblurred by air.

There was the Lunar Observatory, from which Earth and the inner planets could be studied; a silent world in whose sky the home planet hung suspended.

Mercury Observatory, closest to the Sun, perched at Mercury's north pole, where the terminator moved scarcely at all, and the Sun was fixed on the horizon and could be studied in the minutest detail.

Ceres Observatory, newest, most modern, with its range extending from Jupiter to the outermost galaxies.

There were disadvantages, of course. With interplanetary travel still difficult, leaves would be few, anything like normal life virtually impossible, but this was a lucky generation. Coming scientists would find the fields of knowledge well reaped and, until the invention of an interstellar drive, no new horizon as capacious as this one would be opened.

These lucky four, Talliaferro, Ryger, Kaunas, and Villiers, were to be in the position of a Galileo, who, by virtue of owning the first real telescope, could not point it anywhere in the sky without making a major discovery.

But then Romano Villiers had fallen sick and it was rheumatic fever. Whose fault was that? His heart had been left leaking and limping.

He was the most brilliant of the four, the most hopeful, the most intense – and he could not even finish his schooling and get his doctorate.

Worse than that, he could never leave Earth; the acceleration of a spaceship's takeoff would kill him.

Talliaferro was marked for the Moon, Ryger for Ceres, Kaunas for Mercury. Only Villiers stayed behind, a life prisoner of Earth.

They had tried telling their pity and Villiers had rejected it with something approaching hate. He had railed at them and cursed them. When Ryger lost his temper and lifted his fist, Villiers had sprung at him screaming and broken his nose.

Obviously Ryger hadn't forgotten that, as he caressed his nose gingerly with one finger.

Kaunas' forehead was an uncertain washboard of wrinkles. 'He's at the Convention, you know. He's got a room in the hotel – 405.'

'*I* won't see him,' said Ryger.

'He's coming up here. He said he wanted to see us. I thought he said nine. He'll be here any minute.'

'In that case,' said Ryger, 'if you don't mind, I'm leaving.'

Talliaferro said, 'Oh, wait awhile. What's the harm in seeing him?'

'Because there's no point. He's insane.'

'Even so. Let's not be petty about it. Are you afraid of him?'

'Afraid!' Ryger looked contemptuous.

'Nervous, then. What is there to be so nervous about?'

'I'm not nervous,' said Ryger.

'Sure you are. We all feel guilty about him, and without real reason. Nothing that happened was our fault.' But he was speaking defensively and he knew it.

And when, at that point, the door signal sounded, all three jumped and turned to stare uneasily at the barrier that stood between themselves and Villiers.

The door opened and Romano Villiers walked in. The others rose stiffly to greet him, then remained standing in embarrassment, without one hand being raised.

He stared them down sardonically.

He's changed, thought Talliaferro.

He had. He had shrunk in almost every dimension. A gathering stoop even made him seem shorter. The skin of his scalp glistened through thinning hair, the skin on the back of his hands was ridged crookedly with bluish veins. He looked ill. There seemed nothing to link him to the memory of the past except for his trick of shading his eyes with one hand when he stared intently and, when he spoke, the even, controlled baritone of his voice.

He said, 'My friends! My space-trotting friends! We've lost touch.'

Talliaferro said, 'Hello Villiers.'

Villiers eyed him. 'Are you well?'

'Well enough.'

'And you two?'

Kaunas managed a weak smile and a murmur. Ryger snapped, 'All right, Villiers. What's up?'

'Ryger, the angry man,' said Villiers. 'How's Ceres?'

'It was doing well when I left. How's Earth?'

'You can see for yourself,' but Villiers tightened as he said that.

He went on, 'I am hoping that the reason all three of you have come to the Convention is to hear my paper day after tomorrow.'

'Your paper? What paper?' asked Talliaferro.

'I wrote you all about it. My method of mass transference.'

Ryger smiled with one corner of his mouth. 'Yes, you did. You didn't say anything about a paper, though, and I don't recall that you're listed as one of the speakers. I would have noticed it if you had been.'

'You're right. I'm not listed. Nor have I prepared an abstract for publication.'

Villiers had flushed and Talliaferro said soothingly, 'Take it easy, Villiers. You don't look well.'

Villiers whirled on him, lips contorted. 'My heart's holding out, thank you.'

Kaunas said, 'Listen, Villiers, if you're not listed or abstracted —'

'*You* listen. I've waited ten years. You have the jobs in space and I have to teach school on Earth, but I'm a better man than any of you or all of you.'

'Granted —' began Talliaferro.

'And I don't want your condescensions, either. Mandel witnessed it. I suppose you've heard of Mandel. Well, he's chairman of the astronautics division at the Convention and I demonstrated mass transference for him. It was a crude device and it burned out after one use but — Are you listening?'

'We're listening,' said Ryger coldly. 'For what that counts.'

'He'll let me talk about it my way. You bet he will. No warning. No advertisement. I'm going to spring it at them like a bombshell. When I give them the fundamental relationships involved it will break up the Convention. They'll scatter to their home labs to check on me and build devices. And they'll find it works. I made a live mouse disappear at one spot in my lab and appear in another. Mandel witnessed it.'

He stared at them, glaring first at one face, then at another. He said, 'You don't believe me, do you?'

Ryger said, 'If you don't want advertisement, why do you tell us?'

'You're different. You're my friends, my classmates. You went out into space and left me behind.'

86

'That wasn't a matter of choice,' objected Kaunas in a thin, high voice.

Villiers ignored that. He said, 'So I want you to know *now*. What will work for a mouse will work for a human. What will move something ten feet across a lab will move it a million miles across space. I'll be on the Moon, *and* on Mercury, *and* on Ceres and anywhere I want to go. I'll match every one of you and more. And I'll have done more for astronomy just teaching school and thinking than all of you with your observatories and telescopes and cameras and spaceships.'

'Well,' said Talliaferro, 'I'm pleased. More power to you. May I see a copy of the paper?'

'Oh no.' Villiers' hands clenched close to his chest as though he were holding phantom sheets and shielding them from observation. 'You wait like everyone else. There's only one copy and no one will see it till I'm ready. Not even Mandel.'

'One copy!' cried Talliaferro. 'If you misplace it —'

'I won't. And if I do, it's all in my head.'

'If you' – Talliaferro almost finished that sentence with 'die' but stopped himself. Instead, he went on after an almost imperceptible pause – 'have any sense, you'll scan it at least. For safety's sake.'

'No,' said Villiers shortly. 'You'll hear me day after tomorrow. You'll see the human horizon expanded at one stroke as it never has been before.'

Again he stared intently at each face. 'Ten years,' he said. 'Good-bye.'

'He's mad,' said Ryger explosively, staring at the door as though Villiers were still standing before it.

'Is he?' said Talliaferro thoughtfully. 'I suppose he is, in a way. He hates us for irrational reasons. And, then, not even to scan his paper as a precaution . . .'

Talliaferro fingered his own small scanner as he said that. It was just a neutrally colored, undistinguished cylinder, somewhat thicker and somewhat shorter than an ordinary pencil. In recent years it had become the hallmark of the scientist, much as the stethoscope was that of the physician and the microcomputer that of the statistician. The scanner was worn in a jacket pocket, or clipped to a sleeve, or slipped behind the ear or swung at the end of a string.

Talliaferro sometimes, in his more philosophical moments, wondered how it was in the days when research men had to make laborious notes of the literature or file away full-sized reprints. How unwieldy!

Now it was only necessary to scan anything printed or written to have a micronegative which could be developed at leisure. Talliaferro had already recorded every abstract included in the program booklet of the Convention. The other two, he assumed with full confidence, had done likewise.

Talliaferro said, 'Under the circumstances, refusal to scan is mad.'

'Space!' said Ryger hotly. 'There is no paper. There is no discovery. Scoring one on us would be worth any lie to him.'

'But then what will he do day after tomorrow?' asked Kaunas.

'How do I know? He's a madman.'

Talliaferro still played with his scanner and wondered idly if he ought to remove and develop some of the small slivers of film that lay stored away in its vitals. He decided against it. He said, 'Don't underestimate Villiers. He's a brain.'

'Ten years ago, maybe,' said Ryger. 'Now he's a nut. I propose we forget him.'

He spoke loudly, as though to drive away Villiers and all that concerned him by the sheer force with which he discussed other things. He talked about Ceres and his work – the radio plotting of the Milky Way with new radioscopes capable of the resolution of single stars.

Kaunas listened and nodded, then chimed in with information concerning the radio emissions of sunspots and his own paper, in press, on the association of proton storms with the gigantic hydrogen flares on the Sun's surface.

Talliaferro contributed little. Lunar work was unglamorous in comparison. The latest information on long-scale weather forecasting through direct observation of terrestrial jet streams would not compare with radioscopes and proton storms.

More than that, his thoughts could not leave Villiers. Villiers *was* the brain. They all knew it. Even Ryger, for all his bluster, must feel that if mass transference were at all possible then Villiers was a logical discoverer.

The discussion of their own work amounted to no more than an uneasy admission that none of them had come to much. Talliaferro had followed the literature and knew. His own papers had been minor. The others had authored nothing of great importance.

None of them – face the fact – had developed into space shakers. The colossal dreams of schooldays had not come true and that was that. They were competent routine workmen. No more than that, they knew.

Villiers would have been more. They knew that, too. It was that knowledge, as well as guilt, which kept them in antagonism.

Talliaferro felt uneasily that Villiers, despite everything, was yet to *be* more. The others must be thinking so too, and mediocrity could grow quickly unbearable. The mass transference paper would come to pass and Villiers would be the great man after all, as he was always fated to be apparently, while his classmates, with all their advantages, would be forgotten. Their role would be no more than to applaud from the crowd.

He felt his own envy and chagrin and was ashamed of it, but felt it nonetheless.

Conversation died, and Kaunas said, his eyes turning away, 'Listen, why don't we drop in on old Villiers?'

There was a false heartiness about it, a completely unconvincing effort at casualness. He added, 'No use leaving bad feelings . . .'

Talliaferro thought. He wants to make sure about the mass transference. He's hoping it *is* only a madman's nightmare so he can sleep tonight.

But he was curious himself, so he made no objection, and even Ryger shrugged with ill grace and said, 'Hell, why not?'

It was then a little before eleven.

Talliaferro was awakened by the insistent ringing of his door signal. He hitched himself to one elbow in the darkness and felt distinctly outraged. The soft glow of the ceiling indicator showed it to be not quite four in the morning.

He cried out, 'Who is it?'

The ringing continued in spurts.

Growling, Talliaferro slipped into his bathrobe. He opened the door and blinked in the corridor light. He recognized the man who faced him from the trimensionals he had seen often enough.

Nevertheless the man said in an abrupt whisper, 'My name is Hubert Mandel.'

'Yes, sir,' said Talliaferro. Mandel was one of the Names in astronomy, prominent enough to have an important executive position with the World Astronomical Bureau, active enough to be Chairman of the astronautics section here at the Convention.

It suddenly struck Talliaferro that it was Mandel for whom Villiers claimed to have demonstrated mass transference. The thought of Villiers was somehow a sobering one.

Mandel said, 'You are Dr. Edward Talliaferro?'

'Yes, sir.'

'Then dress and come with me. It is very important. It concerns a common acquaintance.'

'Dr. Villiers?'

Mandel's eyes flickered a bit. His brows and lashes were so fair as to give those eyes a naked, unfringed appearance. His hair was silky thin, his age about fifty.

He said, 'Why Villiers?'

'He mentioned you last evening. I don't know any other common acquaintance.'

Mandel nodded, waited for Talliaferro to finish slipping into his clothes, then turned and led the way. Ryger and Kaunas were waiting in a room one floor above Talliaferro's. Kaunas' eyes were red and troubled. Ryger was smoking a cigarette with impatient puffs.

Talliaferro said. 'We're all here. Another reunion.' It fell flat.

He took a seat and the three stared at one another. Ryger

90

shrugged.

Mandel paced the floor, hands deep in his pockets. He said, 'I apologize for any inconvenience, gentlemen, and I thank you for your cooperation. I would like more of it. Our friend Romano Villiers is dead. About an hour ago, his body was removed from the hotel. The medical judgment is heart failure.'

There was a stunned silence. Ryger's cigarette hovered halfway to his lips, then sank slowly without completing its journey.

'Poor devil,' said Talliaferro.

'Horrible,' whispered Kaunas hoarsely. 'He was ...' His voice played out.

Ryger shook himself. 'Well, he had a bad heart. There's nothing to be done.'

'One little thing,' corrected Mandel quietly. 'Recovery.'

'What does that mean?' asked Ryger sharply.

Mandel said, 'When did you three see him last?'

Talliaferro spoke. 'Last evening. It turned out to be a reunion. We all met for the first time in ten years. It wasn't a pleasant meeting, I'm sorry to say. Villiers felt he had cause for anger with us, and he was angry.'

'That was – when?'

'About nine, the first time.'

'The first time?'

'We saw him again later in the evening.'

Kaunas looked troubled. 'He had stormed off angrily. We couldn't leave it at that. We had to try. It wasn't as if we hadn't all been friends at one time. So we went to his room and —'

Mandel pounced on that. 'You were all in his room?'

'Yes,' said Kaunas, surprised.

'About when?'

'Eleven, I think.' He looked at the others. Talliaferro nodded.

'And how long did you stay?'

'Two minutes,' put in Ryger. 'He ordered us out as though we were after his paper.' He paused as if expecting Mandel to ask what paper, but Mandel said nothing. He went on, 'I think he kept it under his pillow. At least he lay across the

91

pillow as he yelled at us to leave.'

'He may have been dying then,' said Kaunas in a sick whisper.

'Not then,' said Mandel shortly. 'So you probably all left fingerprints.'

'Probably,' said Talliaferro. He was losing some of his automatic respect for Mandel and a sense of impatience was returning. It *was* four in the morning. Mandel or no. He said, 'Now what's all this about?'

'Well, gentlemen,' said Mandel, 'there's more to Villiers' death than the fact of death. Villiers' paper, the only copy of it as far as I know, was stuffed into the flash-disposal unit and only scraps of it were left. I've never seen or read the paper, but I know enough about the matter to be willing to swear in court if necessary that the remnants of unflashed paper in the disposal unit were of the paper he was planning to give at this Convention. You seem doubtful, Dr. Ryger.'

Ryger smiled sourly. 'Doubtful that he was going to give it. If you want my opinion, sir, he was mad. For ten years he was a prisoner of Earth and he fantasied mass transference as escape. It was all that kept him alive probably. He rigged up some sort of fraudulent demonstration. I don't say it was deliberate fraud. He was probably madly sincere, and sincerely mad. Last evening was the climax. He came to our rooms – he hated us for having escaped Earth – and triumphed over us. It was what he had lived for for ten years. It may have shocked him back to some form of sanity. He knew he couldn't actually give the paper; there was nothing to give. So he burned it and his heart gave out. It *is* too bad.'

Mandel listened to the Cerian astronomer, wearing a look of sharp disapproval. He said, 'Very glib, Dr. Ryger, but quite wrong. I am not so easily fooled by fraudulent demonstrations as you may believe. Now according to the registration data, which I have been forced to check rather hastily, you three were his classmates at college. Is that right?'

They nodded.

'Are there any other classmates of yours present at the Convention?'

'No,' said Kaunas. 'We were the only four qualifying for a doctorate in astronomy that year. At least he would have qualified except —'

'Yes, I understand,' said Mandel. 'Well, then, in that case one of you three visited Villiers in his room one last time at midnight.'

There was a short silence. Then Ryger said coldly, 'Not I.' Kaunas, eyes wide, shook his head.

Talliaferro said, 'What are you implying?'

'One of you came to him at midnight and insisted on seeing his paper. I don't know the motive. Conceivably it was with the deliberate intention of forcing him into heart failure. When Villiers collapsed, the criminal, if I may call him so, was ready. He snatched the paper, which, I might add, probably *was* kept under his pillow, and scanned it. Then he destroyed the paper itself in the flash-disposal, but he was in a hurry and destruction wasn't complete.'

Ryger interrupted. 'How do you know all this? Were you a witness?'

'Almost,' said Mandel. 'Villiers was not quite dead at the moment of his first collapse. When the criminal left, he managed to reach the phone and call my room. He choked out a few phrases, enough to outline what had occurred. Unfortunately I was not in my room; a late conference kept me away. However, my recording attachment taped it. I always play the recording tape back whenever I return to my room or office. Bureaucratic habit. I called back. He was dead.'

'Well, then,' said Ryger, 'who did he say did it?'

'He didn't. Or if he did, it was unintelligible. But one word rang out clearly. It was *classmate*.'

Talliaferro detached his scanner from its place in his inner jacket pocket and held it out toward Mandel. Quietly he said, 'If you would like to develop the film in my scanner, you are welcome to do so. You will not find Villiers' paper there.'

At once Kaunas did the same, and Ryger, with a scowl, joined.

Mandel took all three scanners and said dryly, 'Presumably, whichever one of you has done this has already disposed of the piece of exposed film with the paper on it. However —'

Talliaferro raised his eyebrows. 'You may search my person or my room.'

But Ryger was still scowling. 'Now wait a minute, wait one bloody minute. Are you the police?'

Mandel stared at him. 'Do you *want* the police? Do you want a scandal and a murder charge? Do you want the Convention disrupted and the System press making a holiday out of astronomy and astronomers? Villiers' death might well have been accidental. He *did* have a bad heart. Whichever one of you was there may well have acted on impulse. It may not have been a premeditated crime. If whoever it is will return the negative, we can avoid a great deal of trouble.'

'Even for the criminal?' asked Talliaferro.

Mandel shrugged. 'There may be trouble for him. I will not promise immunity. But whatever the trouble, it won't be public disgrace and life imprisonment, as it might be if the police are called in.'

Silence.

Mandel said, 'It is one of you three.'

Silence.

Mandel went on, 'I think I can see the original reasoning of the guilty person. The paper would be destroyed. Only we four knew of the mass transference and only I had ever seen a demonstration. Moreover you had only his word, a madman's word perhaps, that I had seen it. With Villiers dead of heart failure and the paper gone, it would be easy to believe Dr. Ryger's theory that there was no mass transference and never had been. A year or two might pass and our criminal, in possession of the mass transference data, could reveal it little by little, rig experiments, publish careful papers, and end as the apparent discoverer with all that would imply in terms of money and renown. Even his own classmates would suspect nothing. At most they would believe that the long-past affair with Villiers had inspired him to begin investigations in the field. No more.'

Mandel looked sharply from one face to another, 'But none of that will work now. Any of the three of you who comes through with mass transference is proclaiming himself the criminal. I've seen the demonstrations; I know it is legitimate; I know that one of you possesses a record of the paper. The information is therefore useless to you. Give it up then.'

Silence.

Mandel walked to the door and turned again. 'I'd appreciate it if you would stay here till I return. I won't be long. I hope the guilty one will use the interval to consider. If he's afraid a confession will lose him his job, let him remember that a session with the police may lose him his liberty *and* cost him the psychoprobe.' He hefted the three scanners, looked grim and somewhat in need of sleep. 'I'll develop these.'

Kaunos tried to smile. 'What if we make a break for it while you're gone?'

'Only one of you has reason to try,' said Mandel. 'I think I can rely on the two innocent ones to control the third, if only out of self-protection.'

He left.

It was five in the morning. Ryger looked at his watch indignantly. 'A hell of a thing. I want to sleep.'

'We can curl up here,' said Talliaferro philosophically. 'Is anyone planning a confession?'

Kaunas looked away and Ryger's lip lifted.

'I didn't think so.' Talliaferro closed his eyes, leaned his large head back against the chair, and said in a tired voice, 'Back on the Moon, they're in the slack season. We've got a two-week night and then it's busy, busy. Then there's two weeks of Sun and there's nothing but calculations, correlations, and bull sessions. That's the hard time. I hate it. If there were more women, if I could arrange something permanent ...'

In a whisper, Kaunas talked about the fact that it was still impossible to get the entire Sun above the horizon and in view of the telescope on Mercury. But, with another two miles of track soon to be laid down for the observatory – move the whole thing, you know, tremendous forces involved, solar energy used directly – it might be managed. It *would* be managed.

Even Ryger consented to talk of Ceres after listening to

the low murmur of the other voices. There was the problem there of the two-hour rotation period, which meant the stars whipped across the sky at an angular velocity twelve times that in Earth's sky. A net of three light scopes, three radioscopes, three of everything, caught the fields of study from one another as they whirled past.

'Could you use one of the poles?' asked Kaunas.

'You're thinking of Mercury and the Sun,' said Ryger, impatiently. 'Even at the poles the sky would still twist, and half of it would be forever hidden. Now if Ceres showed only one face to the Sun, the way Mercury does, we could have a permanent night sky with the stars rotating slowly once in three years.'

The sky lightened and it dawned slowly.

Talliaferro was half-asleep, but he kept hold of half-consciousness firmly. He would not fall asleep and leave the others awake. Each of the three, he thought, was wondering, 'Who? Who?'

Except the guilty one, of course.

Talliaferro's eyes snapped open as Mandel entered again. The sky, as seen from the window, had grown blue. Talliaferro was glad the window was closed. The hotel was air-conditioned, of course, but windows would be opened during the mild seasons of the year by those Earthmen who fancied the illusion of fresh air. Talliaferro, with Moon vacuum on his mind, shuddered at the thought with real discomfort.

Mandel said, 'Have any of you anything to say?'

They looked at him steadily. Ryger shook his head.

Mandel said, 'I have developed the film in your scanners, gentlemen, and viewed the results.' He tossed scanners and developed slivers of film on to the bed. 'Nothing. You'll have trouble sorting out the film, I'm afraid. For that I'm sorry. And now there is still the question of the missing film.'

'If any,' said Ryger, and yawned prodigiously.

Mandel said, 'I would suggest we come down to Villiers' room, gentlemen.'

Kaunas looked startled. 'Why?'

96

Talliaferro said. 'Is this psychology? Bring the criminal to the scene of the crime and remorse will wring a confession from him?'

Mandel said, 'A less melodramatic reason is that I would like to have the two of you who are innocent help me find the missing film of Villiers' paper.'

'Do you think it's there?' asked Ryger challengingly.

'Possibly. It's a beginning. We can then search each of your rooms. The symposium on Astronautics doesn't start till tomorrow at 10 a.m. We have till then.'

'And after that?'

'It may have to be the police.'

They stepped gingerly into Villiers' room. Ryger was red, Kaunas pale. Talliaferro tried to remain calm.

Last night they had seen it under artificial lighting with a scowling, dishevelled Villiers clutching his pillow, staring them down, ordering them away. Now there was the scent-less odour of death about it.

Mandel fiddled with the window polarizer to let more light in and adjusted it too far, so that the eastern Sun slipped in.

Kaunas threw his arm up to shade his eyes and screamed, 'The Sun!' so that all the others froze.

Kaunas' face had gone into a kind of terror, as though it were his Mercurian Sun that he had caught a blinding glimpse of.

Talliaferro thought of his own reaction to the possibility of open air and his teeth gritted. They were all bent crooked by their ten years away from Earth.

Kaunas ran to the window, fumbling for the polarizer, and then the breath came out of him in a huge gasp.

Mandel stepped to his side. 'What's wrong?' and the other two joined them.

The city lay stretched below them and outward to the horizon in broken stone and brick, bathed in the rising Sun, with the shadowed portions toward them. Talliaferro cast it all a furtive and uneasy glance.

Kaunas, his chest seemingly contracted past the point where he could cry out, stared at something much closer.

There, on the outer window sill, one corner secured in a trifling imperfection, a crack in the cement, was an inch-long strip of milky-gray film, and on it were the early rays of the rising Sun.

Mandel, with an angry, incoherent cry, threw up the window and snatched it away. He shielded it in one cupped hand, staring out of hot and reddened eyes.

He said, 'Wait here!'

There was nothing to say. When Mandel left, they sat down and stared stupidly at one another.

Mandel was back in twenty minutes. He said quietly – in a voice that gave the impression, somehow, that it was quiet only because its owner had passed far beyond the raving stage – 'The corner in the crack wasn't overexposed. I could make out a few words. It is Villiers' paper. The rest is ruined; nothing can be salvaged. It's gone.'

'What next?' said Talliaferro.

Mandel shrugged wearily. 'Right now, I don't care. Mass transference is gone until someone as brilliant as Villiers works it out again. I shall work on it, but I have no illusions as to my own capacity. With it gone, I suppose you three don't matter, guilty or not. What's the difference?' His whole body seemed to have loosened and sunk into despair.

But Talliaferro's voice grew hard. 'Now, hold on. In your eyes, any of the three of us might be guilty. I, for instance. You are a big man in the field and you will never have a good word to say for me. The general idea may arise that I am incompetent or worse. I will not be ruined by the shadow of guilt. Now let's solve this thing.'

'I am no detective,' said Mandel wearily.

'Then why don't you call in the police, damn it?'

Ryger said, 'Wait a while, Tal. Are you implying that I'm guilty?'

'I'm only saying that I'm innocent.'

Kaunas raised his voice in fright. 'It will mean the psychoprobe for each of us. There may be mental damage —

Mandel raised both arms high in the air. 'Gentlemen! Gentlemen! Please! There is one thing we might do short of

98

the police; and you are right, Dr. Talliaferro, it would be unfair to the innocent to leave this matter here.'

They turned to him in various stages of hostility. Ryger said, 'What do you suggest?'

'I have a friend named Wendell Urth. You may have heard of him, or you may not, but perhaps I can arrange to see him tonight.'

'What if we can?' demanded Talliaferro. 'Where does that get us?'

'He's an odd man,' said Mandel hesitantly. 'Very odd. And very brilliant in his way. He has helped the police before this and he may be able to help us now.'

Edward Talliaferro could not forbear staring at the room and its occupant with the greatest astonishment. It and he seemed to exist in isolation, and to be part of no recognizable world. The sounds of Earth were absent in this well-padded, windowless nest. The light and air of Earth had been blanked out in artificial illumination and conditioning.

It was a large room, dim and cluttered. They had picked their way across the littered floor to a couch from which book-films had been brusquely cleared and dumped to one side in an amorphous tangle.

The man who owned the room had a large round face on a stumpy round body. He moved quickly about on his short legs, jerking his head as he spoke until his thick glasses all but bounced off the thoroughly inconspicuous nubbin that served in the office of a nose. His thick-lidded, somewhat protuberant eyes gleamed in myopic good nature at them all, as he seated himself in his own chair-desk combination, lit directly by the one bright light in the room.

'So good of you to come, gentlemen. Pray excuse the condition of my room.' He waved stubby fingers in a wide-sweeping gesture. 'I am engaged in cataloguing the many objects of extraterrological interest I have accumulated. It is a tremendous job. For instance —'

He dodged out of his seat and burrowed in a heap of objects beside the desk till he came up with a smoky grey object, semi-translucent and roughly cylindrical. 'This,' he said, 'is a Callistan object that may be a relic of intelligent nonhuman entities. It is not decided. No more than a dozen have been discovered and that is the most perfect single specimen I know of.'

He tossed it to one side and Talliaferro jumped. The plump man stared in his direction and said, 'It's not breakable.' He sat down again, clasped his pudgy fingers tightly over his abdomen and let them pump slowly in and out as he breathed. 'And now what can I do for you?'

Hubert Mandel had carried through the introductions and Talliaferro was considering deeply. Surely it was a man named Wendell Urth who had written a recent book entitled *Comparative Evolutionary Processes on Water–Oxygen Planets,* and surely this could not be the man.

He said, 'Are you the author of *Comparative Evolutionary Processes,* Dr. Urth?'

A beatific smile spread across Urth's face. 'You've read it?'

'Well, no, I haven't, but —'

Urth's expression grew instantly censorious. 'Then you should. Right now. Here, I have a copy.'

He bounced out of his chair again and Mandel cried, 'Now wait, Urth, first things first. This is serious.'

He virtually forced Urth back into his chair and began speaking rapidly as though to prevent any further side issues from erupting. He told the whole story with admirable word economy.

Urth reddened slowly as he listened. He seized his glasses and shoved them higher up on his nose. 'Mass transference!' he cried.

'I saw it with my own eyes,' said Mandel.

'And you never told me.'

'I was sworn to secrecy. The man was ... peculiar. I explained that.'

Urth pounded the desk. 'How could you allow such a discovery to remain the property of an eccentric, Mandel? The knowledge should have been forced from him by psychoprobe, if necessary.'

'It would have killed him,' protested Mandel.

But Urth was rocking back and forth with his hands clasped tightly to his cheeks. 'Mass transference. The only

100

way a decent, civilized man could travel. The only possible way. The only conceivable way. If I had known. If I could have been there. But the hotel is nearly thirty miles away.'

Ryger, who listened with an expression of annoyance on his face, interposed, 'I understand there's a filter line direct to Convention Hall. It could have got you there in ten minutes.'

Urth stiffened and looked at Ryger strangely. His cheeks bulged. He jumped to his feet and scurried out of the room.

Ryger said, 'What the devil?'

Mandel muttered, 'Damn it, I should have warned you.'

'About what?'

'Dr. Urth doesn't travel on any sort of conveyance. It's a phobia. He moves about only on foot.'

Kaunas blinked about in the dimness. 'But he's an extraterrologist, isn't he? An expert on life forms of other planets?'

Talliaferro had risen and now stood before a Galactic Lens on a pedestal. He stared at the inner gleam of the star systems. He had never seen a Lens so large or so elaborate.

Mandel said, 'He's an extraterrologist, yes, but he's never visited any of the planets on which he is expert and he never will. In thirty years, he's never been more than a few miles from this room.'

Ryger laughed.

Mandel flushed angrily. 'You may find it funny, but I'd appreciate your being careful what you say when Dr. Urth comes back.'

Urth sidled in a moment later. 'My apologies, gentlemen,' he said in a whisper. 'And now let us approach our problem. Perhaps one of you wishes to confess?'

Talliaferro's lips quirked sourly. This plump, self-imprisoned extraterrologist was scarcely formidable enough to force a confession from anyone. Fortunately there would be no need of him.

Talliaferro said, 'Dr. Urth, are you connected with the police?'

A certain smugness seemed to suffuse Urth's ruddy face. 'I have no official connection, Dr. Talliaferro, but my unofficial relationships are very good indeed.'

'In that case, I will give you some information which you can carry to the police.'

Urth drew in his abdomen and hitched at his shirttail. It came free and slowly he polished his glasses with it. When he was quite through and had perched them precariously on his nose once more, he said, 'And what is that?'

'I will tell you who was present when Villiers died and who scanned his paper.'

'You have solved the mystery?'

'I've thought about it all day. I think I've solved it.' Talliaferro rather enjoyed the sensation he was creating.

'Well, then?'

Talliaferro took a deep breath. This was not going to be easy to do, though he had been planning it for hours. 'The guilty man,' he said, 'is obviously Dr. Hubert Mandel.'

Mandel stared at Talliaferro in sudden, hard-breathing indignation. 'Look here, Doctor,' he began loudly, 'if you have any basis —'

Urth's tenor voice soared above the interruption. 'Let him talk, Hubert, let us hear him. You suspected him and there is no law that forbids him to suspect you.'

Mandel fell angrily silent.

Talliaferro, not allowing his voice to falter, said, 'It is more than just suspicion, Dr. Urth. The evidence is perfectly plain. Four of us knew about mass transference, but only one of us, Dr. Mandel, had actually seen a demonstration. He *knew* it to be a fact. He *knew* a paper on the subject existed. We three knew only that Villiers was more or less unbalanced. Oh, we might have thought there was just a chance. We visited him at eleven, I think, just to check on that, though none of us actually said so, but he only acted crazier than ever.

'Check special knowledge and motive then on Dr. Mandel's side. Now, Dr. Urth, picture something else. Whoever it was who confronted Villiers at midnight, saw him collapse, and scanned his paper (let's keep him anonymous for a moment) must have been terribly startled to see Villiers apparently come to life again and to hear him talking into the telephone. Our criminal, in the panic of the moment, realized one thing: he must get rid of the one piece of incriminating material evidence.

'He had to get rid of the undeveloped film of the paper and he had to do it in such a way that it would be safe from discovery so that he might pick it up once more if he remained unsuspected. The outer window sill was ideal. Quickly he threw up Villiers' window, placed the strip of film outside, and left. Now, even if Villiers survived or if his telephoning brought results, it would be merely Villiers' word against his own and it would be easy to show that Villiers was unbalanced.'

Talliaferro paused in something like triumph. This would be irrefutable.

Wendell Urth blinked at him and wiggled the thumbs of his clasped hands so that they slapped against his ample shirt front. He said, 'And the significance of all that?'

'The significance is that the window was thrown open and the film placed in open air. Now Ryger has lived for ten years on Ceres, Kaunas on Mercury, I on the Moon – barring short leaves and not many of them. We commented to one another several times yesterday on the difficulty of growing acclimatized to Earth.

'Our work worlds are each airless objects. We never go out in the open without a suit. To expose ourselves to unenclosed space is unthinkable. None of us could have opened the window without a severe inner struggle. Dr. Mandel, however, has lived on Earth exclusively. Opening a window to him is only a matter of a bit of muscular exertion. He could do it. We couldn't. Ergo, he did it.'

Talliaferro sat back and smiled a bit.

'Space, that's it!' cried Ryger with enthusiasm.

'That's not it at all,' roared Mandel, half-rising as though tempted to throw himself at Talliaferro. 'I deny the whole miserable fabrication. What about the record I have of Villiers' phone call? He used the word *classmate*. The entire tape makes it obvious —'

'He was a dying man,' said Talliaferro. 'Much of what he said you admitted was incomprehensible. I ask you, Dr. Mandel, without having heard the tape, if it isn't true that Villiers' voice is distorted past recognition?'

'Well —' said Mandel confused.

'I'm sure it is. There is no reason to suppose, then, that you might not have rigged up the tape in advance, complete with the damning word *classmate*.'

Mandel said, 'Good lord, how would I know there were classmates at the Convention? How would I know they knew about the mass transference?'

'Villiers might have told you. I presume he did.'

'Now, look,' said Mandel, 'you three saw Villiers alive at eleven. The medical examiner, seeing Villiers' body shortly after 3 a.m., declared he had been dead at least two hours. That was certain. The time of death, therefore, was between 11 p.m. and 1 a.m. I was at a late conference last night. I can prove my whereabouts, miles from the hotel, between ten and two, by a dozen witnesses, no one of whom anyone can possibly question. Is that enough for you?'

Talliaferro paused for a moment. Then he went on stubbornly, 'Even so. Suppose you got back to the hotel by two-thirty. You went to Villiers' room to discuss his talk. You found the door open, or you had a duplicate key. Anyway, you found him dead. You seized the opportunity to scan the paper —'

'And if he were already dead, and couldn't make phone calls, why should I hide the film?'

'To remove suspicion. You may have a second copy of the film safe in your possession. For that matter, we have only your own word that the paper was destroyed.'

'Enough. Enough!' cried Urth. 'It is an interesting hypothesis, Dr. Talliaferro, but it falls to the ground of its own weight.'

Talliaferro frowned. 'That's your opinion, perhaps —'

'It would be anyone's opinion. Anyone, that is, with the power of human thought. Don't you see that Hubert Mandel did too much to be the criminal?'

'No,' said Talliaferro.

Wendell Urth smiled benignly. 'As a scientist, Dr. Talliaferro, you undoubtedly know better than to fall in love with your own theories to the exclusion of facts or reasoning. Do me the pleasure of behaving similarly as a detective.

'Consider that if Dr. Mandel had brought about the death of Villiers and faked an alibi, or if he had found Villiers dead and taken advantage of that, how little he would really have had to do! Why scan the paper or even pretend that anyone had done so. He could simply have taken the paper. Who else knew of its existence? Nobody, really. There was no reason to think Villiers told anyone else about it. Villiers was pathologically secretive. There would have been every reason to think that he told no one.

'No one knew Villiers was giving a talk, except Dr. Mandel. It wasn't announced. No abstract was published. Dr. Mandel could have walked off with the paper in perfect confidence.

'Even if he had discovered that Villiers had talked to his classmates about the matter, what of it? What evidence would his classmates have except the word of one whom they are themselves willing to consider a madman?

'By announcing instead that Villiers' paper had been destroyed, by declaring his death to be not entirely natural, by searching for a scanned copy of the film – in short by everything Dr. Mandel has done, he has aroused a suspicion that only he could possibly have aroused when he need only have remained quiet to have committed a perfect crime. If he were the criminal, he would be more stupid, more colossally obtuse than anyone I have ever known. And Dr. Mandel, after all, is none of that.'

Talliaferro thought hard but found nothing to say.

Ryger said, 'Then who did it?'

'One of you three. That's obvious.'

'But which?'

'Oh, that's obvious too. I knew which of you was guilty the moment Dr. Mandel had completed his description of events.'

Talliaferro stared at the plump extraterrologist with distaste. The bluff did not frighten him, but it was affecting the other two. Ryger's lips were thrust out and Kaunas' lower jaw had relaxed moronically. They looked like fish, both of them.

He said, 'Which one, then? Tell us.'

Urth blinked. 'First, I want to make it perfectly plain that the important thing is mass transference. It can still be recovered.'

Mandel, scowling still, said querulously, 'What the devil are you talking about, Urth?'

'The man who scanned the paper probably looked at what he was scanning. I doubt that he had the time or the presence of mind to read it, and if he did, I doubt if he could remember it ... consciously. However, there is the psychoprobe. If he so much as glanced at the paper, what impinged on his retina could be probed.'

There was an uneasy stir.

Urth said at once, 'No need to be afraid of the psychoprobe. Proper handling is safe, particularly if a man offers himself voluntarily. When damage is done, it is usually because of unnecessary resistance, a kind of mental tearing, you know. So if the guilty man will voluntarily confess, place himself in my hands —'

Talliaferro laughed. The sudden noise rang out sharply in the dim quiet of the room. The psychology was so transparent and artless.

Wendell Urth looked almost bewildered at the reaction and stared earnestly at Talliaferro over his glasses. He said, 'I have enough influence with the police to keep the probing entirely confidential.'

Ryger said savagely, 'I didn't do it.'

Kaunas shook his head.

Talliaferro disdained any answer.

Urth sighed. 'Then I shall have to point out the guilty man. It will be traumatic. It will make things harder.' He tightened the grip on his belly and his fingers twitched. 'Dr. Talliaferro indicated that the film was hidden on the outer window sill so that it might remain safe from discovery and from harm. I agree with him.'

'Thank you,' said Talliaferro dryly.

'However, why should anyone think that an outer window sill is a particularly safe hiding place? The police would certainly look there.

'Even in the absence of the police it was discovered. Who would tend to consider anything outside a building as particularly safe? Obviously some person who has lived a long time on an airless world has had it drilled into him that no one goes outside an enclosed place without detailed precautions.

'To someone on the Moon, for instance, anything hidden outside a Lunar Dome would be comparatively safe. Men venture out only rarely and then only on specific business. So he would overcome the hardship of opening a window and exposing himself to what he would subconsciously consider a vacuum for the sake of a safe hiding place. The reflex thought, *Outside an inhabited structure is safe*, would do the trick.'

Talliaferro said between clenched teeth, 'Why do you mention the Moon, Dr. Urth?'

Urth said blandly, 'Only as an example. What I've said so far applies to all three of you. But now comes the crucial point, the matter of the dying night.'

Talliaferro frowned. 'You mean the night Villiers died?'

'I mean any night. See here, even granted that an outer window sill was a safe hiding place, which of you would be mad enough to consider it a safe hiding place *for a piece of unexposed film*? Scanner film isn't very sensitive, to be sure, and is made to be developed under all sorts of hit-and-miss conditions. Diffuse night-time illumination wouldn't seriously affect it, but diffuse daylight would ruin it in a few minutes, and direct sunlight would ruin it at once. Everyone knows that.'

Mandel said, 'Go ahead, Urth. What is this leading to?'

'You're trying to rush me,' said Urth, with a massive pout. 'I want you to see this clearly. The criminal wanted, above all, to keep the film safe. It was his only record of something of supreme value to himself and to the world. Why would he put it where it would inevitably be ruined almost immediately by the morning Sun? Only because he did not expect the morning Sun ever to come. He thought the night, so to speak, was immortal.

'But nights *aren't* immortal. On Earth they die and give way to daytime. Even the six-month polar night is a dying night eventually. The nights on Ceres last only two hours; the nights on the Moon last two weeks. They are dying nights too, and Drs. Talliaferro and Ryger know that day must always come.'

Kaunas rose. 'But wait —'

Wendell Urth faced him full. 'No longer any need to wait, Dr. Kaunas. Mercury is the only sizable object in the Solar System that turns only one face to the Sun. Even taking libration into account, fully three-eighths of its surface is true dark-side and never sees the Sun. The Polar Observatory is at the rim of that dark-side. For ten years you have grown used to the fact that nights are immortal, that a surface in darkness remains eternally in darkness, and so you entrusted unexposed film to Earth's night, forgetting in your excitement that nights must die —'

Kaunas came forward. 'Wait —'

Urth was inexorable. 'I am told that when Mandel adjusted the polarizer in Villiers' room, you screamed at the sunlight.' Was that your ingrained fear of the Mercurian Sun, or your sudden realization of what sunlight meant to your plans? You rushed forward. Was that to adjust the polarizer, or to stare at the ruined film?'

Kaunas fell to his knees. 'I didn't mean it. I wanted to speak to him, only to speak to him, and he screamed and collapsed. I thought he was dead and the paper was under his pillow and it all just followed. One thing led on to another and before I knew it I couldn't get out of it anymore. But I meant none of it. I swear it.'

They had formed a semicircle about him and Wendell Urth stared at the moaning Kaunas with pity in his eyes.

An ambulance had come and gone. Talliaferro finally brought himself to say stiffly to Mandel, 'I hope, sir, there will be no hard feelings for anything said here.'

And Mandel had answered as stiffly, 'I think we had all better forget as much as possible of what has happened during the last twenty-four hours.'

They were standing in the doorway, ready to leave, and Wendell Urth ducked his smiling head and said, 'There's the question of my fee, you know.'

Mandel looked at him with a startled expression.

'Not money,' said Urth at once. 'But when the first mass transference set up for humans is established, I want a trip arranged for me right away.'

Mandel continued to look anxious. 'Now, wait. Trips

through outer space are a long way off.'

Urth shook his head rapidly. 'Not outer space. Not at all. I would like to step across to Lower Falls, New Hampshire.'

'All right. But why?'

Urth looked up. To Talliaferro's outright surprise, the extraterrologist's face wore an expression compounded equally of shyness and eagerness.

Urth said, 'I once – quite a long time ago – knew a girl there. It's been many years – but I sometimes wonder ...'

Afterword

Some readers may realize that this story, first published in 1956, has been overtaken by events. In 1965, astronomers discovered that Mercury does not keep one side always to the Sun, but has a period of rotation of about fifty-four days, so that all parts of it are exposed to sunlight at one time or another.

Well, what can I do except say that I wish astronomers would get things right to begin with?

And I certainly refuse to change the story to suit their whims.

ANNIVERSARY

THE annual ritual was all set. It was the turn of Moore's house this year, of course, and Mrs. Moore and the children had resignedly gone to her mother's for the evening.

Warren Moore surveyed the room with a faint smile. Only Mark Brandon's enthusiasm kept it going at the first, but he himself had come to like this mild remembrance. It came with age, he supposed; twenty additional years of it. He had grown paunchy, thin-haired, soft-jowled, and – worst of all – sentimental.

So all the windows were polarized into complete darkness and the drapes were drawn. Only occasional stipples of wall were illuminated, thus celebrating the poor lighting and the terrible isolation of that day of wreckage long ago.

There were spaceship rations in sticks and tubes on the table and, of course, in the center an unopened bottle of sparkling green *Jabra* water, the potent brew that only the chemical activity of Martian fungi could supply.

Moore looked at his watch. Brandon would be here soon; he was never late for this occasion. The only thing that disturbed him was the memory of Brandon's voice on the tube: 'Warren, I have a surprise for you this time. Wait and see. Wait and see.'

Brandon, it always seemed to Moore, aged little. The younger man had kept his slimness, and the intensity with which he greeted all in life, to the verge of his fortieth birthday. He retained the ability to be in high excitement over the good and in deep despair over the bad. His hair was going gray, but except for that, when Brandon walked up and down, talking rapidly at the top of his voice about anything at all, Moore didn't even have to close his eyes to see the panicked youngster on the wreck of the *Silver Queen*.

The door-signal sounded and Moore kicked the release without turning round. 'Come, Mark.'

110

It was a strange voice that answered, though; softly, tentatively, 'Mr. Moore?'

Moore turned quickly. Brandon was there, to be sure, but only in the background, grinning with excitement. Someone else was standing before him; short, squat, quite bald, nutbrown and with the feel of space about him.

Moore said wonderingly, 'Mike Shea – *Mike Shea*, by all Space.'

They pounded hands together, laughing.

Brandon said, 'He got in touch with me through the office. He remembered I was with Atomic Products —'

'It's been *years*,' said Moore. 'Let's see, you were on Earth twelve years ago —'

'He's never been here on an anniversary,' said Brandon. 'How about that? He's retiring now. Getting out of space to a place he's buying in Arizona. He came to say hello before he left; stopped off at the city just for that, and I was sure he came for the anniversary. "What anniversary?" says the old jerk.'

Shea nodded, grinning. 'He said you made a kind of celebration out of it every year.'

'You bet,' said Brandon, enthusiastically, 'and this will be the first one with all three of us here, the first *real* anniversary. It's twenty years, Mike; twenty years since Warren scrambled over what was left of the wreck and brought us down to Vesta.'

Shea looked about. 'Space-ration, eh? That's old-home-week to me. And *Jabra*. Oh sure, I remember.... Twenty years. I never give it a thought and now, all of a sudden, it's yesterday. Remember when we got back to Earth finally?'

'Do I!' said Brandon. 'The parades. The speeches. Warren was the only real hero of the occasion and we kept saying so, and they kept paying no attention. Remember?'

'Oh well,' said Moore. 'We were the first three men ever to survive a spaceship crash. We were unusual and anything unusual is worth a celebration. These things are irrational.'

'Hey,' said Shea, 'any of you remember the songs they wrote. That marching one? "You can sing of routes through Space and the weary maddened pace of the —"'

Brandon joined in with his clear tenor and even Moore

111

added his voice to the chorus so that the last line was loud enough to shake the drapes. 'On the *wreck* of the *Silver* Que-e-en,' they roared out and ended laughing wildly.

Brandon said, 'Let's open the *Jabra* for the first little sip. This one bottle has to last all of us all night.'

Moore said, 'Mark insists on complete authenticity. I'm surprised he doesn't expect me to climb out the window and human-fly my way around the building.'

'Well, now, that's an idea,' said Brandon.

'Remember that last toast we made?' Shea held his empty glass before him and intoned, ' "Gentlemen, I give you the year's supply of good old H_2O *we used to have*." Three drunken bums when we landed. – Well, we were kids. I was thirty and I thought I was old. And now,' his voice was suddenly wistful, 'they've retired me.'

'Drink!' said Brandon. 'Today you're thirty again, and we remember the day on the *Silver Queen* even if no one else does. Dirty, fickle public.'

Moore laughed. 'What do you expect? A national holiday every year with space-ration and *Jabra* the ritual food and drink?'

'Listen, we're still the only men ever to survive a space-ship crash and now look at us. We're in oblivion.'

'It's pretty good oblivion. We had a good time to begin with and the publicity gave us a healthy boost up the ladder. We are doing well, Mark. And so would Mike Shea be if he hadn't wanted to return to space.'

Shea grinned and shrugged his shoulder. 'That's where I like to be. I'm not sorry, either. What with the insurance compensation I got, I have a nice piece of cash now to retire on.'

Brandon said reminiscently, 'The wreck set back Trans-space Insurance a real packet. Just the same, there's still something missing. You say *"Silver Queen"* to anyone these days, and he can only think of Quentin, if he can think of anyone.'

'Who?' said Shea.

'Quentin. Dr. Horace Quentin. He was one of the non-survivors on the ship. You say to anyone, "What about the

112

three men who survived?" and they'll just stare at you. "Huh," they'll say.'

Moore said, calmly, 'Come, Mark, face it. Dr. Quentin was one of the world's great scientists and we three are just three of the world's nothings.'

'We survived. We're still the only men on record to survive.'

'So? Look, John Hester was on the ship, and he was an important scientist, too; not in Quentin's league, but important. As a matter of fact, I was next to him at the last dinner before the rock hit us. Well, just because Quentin died in the same wreck, Hester's death was drowned out. No one ever remembers Hester died on the *Silver Queen*. They only remember Quentin. We may be forgotten, too, but at last we're alive.'

'I tell you what,' said Brandon, after a period of silence during which Moore's rationale had obviously failed to take. 'We're marooned again. Twenty years ago today, we were marooned off Vesta. Today, we're marooned in oblivion. Now here are the three of us back together again at last, and what happened before can happen again. Twenty years ago, Warren pulled us down to Vesta. Now let's solve this new problem.'

'Wipe out the oblivion, you mean?' said Moore. 'Make ourselves famous?'

'Sure. Why not? Do you know of any better way of celebrating a twentieth anniversary?'

'No, but I'd be interested to know where you expect to start. I don't think people remember the *Silver Queen* at all, except for Quentin, so you'll have to think of some way of bringing the wreck back to mind. That's just to begin with.'

Shea stirred uneasily and a thoughtful expression crossed his blunt countenance. 'Some people remember the *Silver Queen*. The insurance company does, and you know that's a funny thing, now that you bring up the matter. I was on Vesta about ten-eleven years ago, and I asked if the piece of the wreck we brought down was still there and they said sure, who would cart it away? So I thought I'd take a look

113

at it and shot over by reaction motor strapped to my back. With Vestan gravity, you know, a reaction motor is all you need. Anyway, I didn't get to see it except from a distance. It was circled off by force-field.'

Brandon's eyebrows went skyhigh. 'Our *Silver Queen*? For what reason?'

'I went back and asked how come they didn't tell me, and they said they didn't know I was going there. They said it belonged to the insurance company.'

Moore nodded. 'Surely. They took over when they paid off. I signed a release, giving up my salvage rights when I accepted the compensation check. You did too, I'm sure.'

Brandon said, 'But why the force-field? Why all the privacy?'

'I don't know?'

'The wreck isn't worth anything even as scrap metal. It would cost too much to transport it.'

Shea said, 'That's right. Funny thing, though; they were bringing pieces back from space. There was a pile of it there. I could see it and it looked like just junk, twisted pieces of frame, you know. I asked about it and they said ships were always landing and unloading more scrap, and the insurance company had a standard price for any piece of the *Silver Queen* brought back, so ships in the neighborhood of Vesta were always looking. Then, on my last voyage in, I went to see the *Silver Queen* again and that pile was a lot bigger.'

'You mean they're still looking?' Brandon's eyes glittered.

'I don't know. Maybe they've stopped, but the pile was bigger than it was ten-eleven years ago, so they were still looking then.'

Brandon leaned back in his chair and crossed his legs. 'Well, now, that's very queer. A hard-headed insurance company is spending all kinds of money, sweeping space near Vesta trying to find pieces of a twenty-year-old wreck.'

'Maybe they're trying to prove sabotage,' said Moore.

'After twenty years? They won't get their money back even if they do. It's a dead issue.'

'They may have quit looking years ago.'

Brandon stood up with decision. 'Let's ask. There's something funny here and I'm just *Jabrified* enough and anniver-saried enough to want to find out.'

'Sure,' said Shea, 'but ask who?'

'Ask Multivac,' said Brandon.

Shea's eyes opened wide. 'Multivac! Say, Mr. Moore, do you have a Multivac outlet here?'

'Yes.'

'I've never seen one, and I've always wanted to.'

'It's nothing to look at, Mike. It just looks like a type-writer. Don't confuse a Multivac outlet with Multivac itself. I don't know anyone who's seen Multivac.'

Moore smiled at the thought. He doubted if ever in his life he would meet any of the handful of technicians that spent most of their working days in a hidden spot in the bowels of Earth tending a mile-long super-computer that was the repository of all the facts known to man; that guided man's economy; directed his scientific research; helped make his political decisions – and had millions of circuits left over to answer individual questions that did not violate the ethics of privacy.

Brandon said as they moved up the power-ramp to the second floor, 'I've been thinking of installing a Multivac, Jr. outlet for the kids. Homework and things, you know. And yet I don't want to make it just a fancy and expensive crutch for them. How do you work it, Warren?'

Moore said, tersely, 'They show me the questions first. If I don't pass them, Multivac does not see them.'

The Multivac outlet was indeed a simple typewriter ar-rangement and little more.

Moore set up the co-ordinates that opened his portion of the planet-wide network of circuits and said, 'Now listen. For the record, I'm against this and I'm only going along because it's the anniversary and because I'm just jackass enough to be curious. Now how ought I to phrase the question?'

Brandon said, 'Just ask: Are pieces of the wreck of the *Silver Queen* still being searched for in the neighborhood of Vesta by Trans-space Insurance? It only requires a simple yes or no.'

Moore shrugged and tapped it out, while Shea watched with awe.

The spaceman said, 'How does it answer? Does it talk?'

Moore laughed gently. 'Oh, no. I don't spend *that* kind of money. This model just prints the answer on a slip of tape that comes out that slot.'

A short strip of tape did come out as he spoke. Moore removed it and after a glance, said, 'Well, Multivac says yes.'

'Hah!' cried Brandon. 'Told you. Now ask why?'

'Now that's silly. A question like that would be obviously against privacy. You'll just get a yellow state-your-reason.'

'Ask and find out. They have not made the search for the pieces secret. Maybe they're not making the reason secret.'

Moore shrugged. He tapped out: Why is Trans-space Insurance conducting its *Silver Queen* search-project to which reference was made in the previous question?

A yellow slip clicked out almost at once: *State Your Reason For Requiring The Information Requested.*

'All right,' said Brandon, unabashed. 'You tell it we're the three survivors and have a right to know. Go ahead. Tell it.'

Moore tapped that out in unemotional phrasing and another yellow slip was pushed out at them: *Your Reason Is Insufficient. No Answer Can Be Given.*

Brandon said, 'I don't see they have a right to keep that secret.'

'That's up to Multivac,' said Moore. 'It judges the reasons given it and if it decides the ethics of privacy is against answering, that's it. The government itself couldn't break those ethics without a court order, and the courts don't go against Multivac once in ten years. So what are you going to do?'

Brandon jumped to his feet and began the rapid walk up and down the room that was so characteristic of him. 'All right, then let's figure it out for ourselves. It's something important to justify all their trouble. We're agreed they're not trying to find evidence of sabotage, not after twenty years. But Trans-space must be looking for *something*;

something so valuable that it's worth looking for all this time. Now what could be that valuable?'

'Mark, you're a dreamer,' said Moore.

Brandon obviously didn't hear him. 'It can't be jewels or money or securities. There just couldn't be enough to pay them back for what the search has already cost them; not if the *Silver Queen* were pure gold. What would be more valuable?'

'You can't judge value, Mark,' said Moore. 'A letter might be worth a hundredth of a cent as waste-paper and yet make a difference of a hundred million dollars to a corporation, depending on what's in the letter.'

Brandon nodded his head vigorously. 'Right. Documents. Valuable papers. Now who would be most likely to have papers worth billions in his possession on that trip?'

'How could anyone possibly say?'

'How about Dr. Horace Quentin? How about that, Warren? He's the one people remember because he was so important. What about the papers he might have had with him; details of a new discovery, maybe. Damn it, if I had only seen him on that trip. He might have told me something, just in casual conversation, you know. Did *you* ever see him, Warren?'

'Not that I recall. Not to talk to. So casual conversation with me is out, too. Of course, I might have passed him at some time without knowing it.'

'No, you wouldn't have,' said Shea, suddenly thoughtful. 'I think I remember something. There was one passenger who never left his cabin. The steward was talking about it. He wouldn't even come out for meals.'

'And that was Quentin?' said Brandon, stopping his pacing and staring at the spaceman eagerly.

'It might have been, Mr. Brandon. It might have been him. I don't know that anyone *said* it was. I don't remember. But it must have been a big shot, because on a spaceship you don't fool around bringing meals to a man's cabin unless he *is* a big shot.'

'And Quentin was *the* big shot on the trip,' said Brandon, with satisfaction. 'So he had something in his cabin. Something very important. Something he was concealing.'

117

'He might just have been space-sick,' said Moore, 'except that —' He frowned and fell silent.

'Go ahead,' said Brandon, urgently. 'You remember something, too?'

'Maybe. I told you I was sitting next to Dr. Hester at the last dinner. He was saying something about hoping to meet Dr. Quentin on the trip and not having any luck.'

'Sure,' cried Brandon, 'because Quentin wouldn't come out of his cabin.'

'He didn't *say* that. We got to talking about Quentin, though. Now what was it he said?' Moore put his hands to his temples as though trying to squeeze out the memory of twenty years ago by main force. 'I can't give you the exact words, of course, but it was something about Quentin being very theatrical or a slave of drama or something like that, and they were heading out to some scientific conference on Ganymede and Quentin wouldn't even announce the title of his paper.'

'It all fits.' Brandon resumed his rapid pacing. 'He had a new, great discovery, which he was keeping absolutely secret, because he was going to spring it on the Ganymede conference and get maximum drama out of it. He wouldn't come out of his cabin because he probably thought Hester would pump him – and Hester would, I'll bet. And then the ship hit the rock and Quentin was killed. Trans-space Insurance investigated, got rumors of this new discovery and figured that if they gained control of it, they could make back their losses and plenty more. So they took ownership of the ship and have been hunting for Quentin's papers among the pieces ever since.'

Moore smiled, in absolute affection for the other man. 'Mark, that's a beautiful theory. The whole evening is worth it, just watching you make something out of nothing.'

'Oh yeah. Something out of nothing? Let's ask Multivac again. I'll pay the bill for it this month.'

'It's all right. Be my guest. If you don't mind, though, I'm going to bring up the bottle of *Jabra*. I want one more little shot to catch up with you.'

'Me, too,' said Shea.

Brandon took his seat at the typewriter. His fingers trembled with eagerness as he tapped out: What was the nature of Dr. Horace Quentin's final investigations?

Moore had returned with the bottle and glasses, when the answer came back; on white paper this time. The answer was long and the print was fine, consisting for the most part of references to scientific papers in journals twenty years old.

Moore went over it. 'I'm no physicist, but it looks to me as though he were interested in optics.'

Brandon shook his head impatiently. 'But all that is published. We want something he had not published yet.'

'We'll never find out anything about that.'

'The insurance company did.'

'That's just your theory.'

Brandon was kneading his chin with an unsteady hand. 'Let me ask Multivac one more question.'

He sat down again and tapped out: 'Give me the name and tube-number of the surviving colleagues of Dr. Horace Quentin from among those associated with him at the university on whose faculty he served.'

'How do you know he was on a university faculty?' asked Moore.

'If not, Multivac will tell us.'

A slip popped out. It contained only one name.

Moore said, 'Are you planning to call the man?'

'I sure am,' said Brandon. '– Otis Fitzimmons, with a Detroit tube-number. Warren, may I —'

'Be my guest, Mark. It's still part of the game.'

Brandon set up the combination on Moore's tube keyboard. A woman's voice answered. Brandon asked for Dr. Fitzimmons and there was a short wait.

Then a thin voice said, 'Hello.' It sounded old.

Brandon said, 'Dr. Fitzimmons, I'm representing Transspace Insurance in the matter of the late Dr. Horace Quentin —'

('For heaven's sake, Mark,' whispered Moore, but Brandon held up a sharply restraining hand.)

There was a pause so long that a tube breakdown began to seem possible and then the old voice said, 'After all these years? Again?'

(Brandon snapped his fingers in an irrepressible gesture of triumph.)

But he said smoothly, almost glibly, 'We're still trying to find out, Doctor, if you have remembered further details about what Dr. Quentin might have had with him on that last trip that would pertain to his last unpublished discovery.'

'Well —' There was an impatient clicking of the tongue. 'I've told you, I don't know. I don't want to be bothered with this again. I don't know that there was *anything*. The man hinted, but he was always hinting about some gadget or other.'

'What gadget, sir?'

'I tell you I don't know. He used a name once and I told you about that. I don't think it's significant.'

'We don't have the name in our records, sir.'

'Well, you should have. Uh, what was that name? An optikon, that's it.'

'With a *k*?'

'*C* or *k*. I don't know or care. Now, please, I do not wish to be disturbed again about this. Good-bye.' He was still mumbling querulously, when the line went dead.

Brandon was pleased.

Moore said, 'Mark, that was the stupidest thing you could have done. Claiming a fraudulent identity on the tube is illegal. If he wants to make trouble for you —'

'Why should he? He's forgotten about it already. But don't you see, Warren? Trans-space has been asking him about this. He kept saying he'd explained all this before.'

'All right. But you'd assumed that much. What else do you know?'

'We also know,' said Brandon, 'that Quentin's gadget was called an optikon.'

'Fitzimmons didn't sound certain about that. And even so, since we already know he was specializing in optics toward the end, a name like "optikon" does not push us any further forward.'

'And Trans-space Insurance is looking either for the optikon or for papers concerning it. Maybe Quentin kept the details in his hat and just had a model of the instrument. After all, Shea said they were picking up metal objects. Right?'

'There was a bunch of metal junk in the pile,' agreed Shea.

'They'd leave that in space if it were papers they were after. So that's what we want, an instrument that might be called an optikon.'

'Even if all your theories were correct, Mark, and we're looking for an optikon, the search is absolutely hopeless now,' said Moore, flatly. 'I doubt that more than ten percent of the debris would remain in orbit about Vesta. Vesta's escape velocity is practically nothing. It was just a lucky thrust in a lucky direction and at a lucky velocity that put our section of the wreck in orbit. The rest is gone, scattered all over the Solar system in any conceivable orbit about the Sun.'

'They've been picking up pieces,' said Brandon.

'Yes, the ten per cent that managed to make a Vestan orbit out of it. That's all.'

Brandon wasn't giving up. He said thoughtfully, 'Suppose it *were* there and they hadn't found it. Could someone have beat them to it?'

Mike Shea laughed. 'We were right there, but we sure didn't walk off with anything but our skins, and glad to do that much. Who else?'

'That's right,' agreed Moore, 'and if anyone else picked it up, why are they keeping it a secret?'

'Maybe they don't know what it is.'

'Then how do we go about —' Moore broke off and turned to Shea, 'What did you say?'

Shea looked blank. 'Who me?'

'Just now, about us being there.' Moore's eyes narrowed. He shook his head as though to clear it, then whispered, 'Great Galaxy!'

'What is it?' asked Brandon, tensely. 'What's the matter, Warren?'

'I'm not sure. You're driving me mad with your theories; so mad, I'm beginning to take them seriously, I think. You know, we *did* take some things out of the wreck with us. I mean besides our clothes and what personal belongings we still had. Or at least I did.'

'What?'

'It was when I was making my way across the outside of the wreckage – Space, I seem to be there now, I see it so clearly – I picked up some items and put them in the pocket of my spacesuit. I don't know why; I wasn't myself, really. I did it without thinking. And then, well, I held on to them. Souvenirs, I suppose. I brought them back to Earth.'

'Where are they?'

'I don't know. We haven't stayed in one place, you know.'

'You didn't throw them out, did you?'

'No, but things do get lost when you move.'

'If you didn't throw them out, they must be somewhere in this house.'

'If they didn't get lost. I swear I don't recall seeing them in fifteen years.'

'What were they?'

Warren Moore said, 'One was a fountain pen, as I recall; a real antique, the kind that used an ink-spray cartridge. What gets me, though, is that the other was a small field-glass, not more than about six inches long. You see what I mean? A field-glass?'

'An optikon,' shouted Brandon. 'Sure!'

'It's just a coincidence,' said Moore, trying to remain level-headed. 'Just a curious coincidence.'

But Brandon wasn't having it. 'A coincidence, nuts! Trans-space couldn't find the optikon on the wreck and they couldn't find it in space because you had it all along.'

'You're crazy.'

'Come on, we've got to find the thing now.'

Moore blew out his breath. 'Well, I'll look, if that's what you want, but I doubt that I'll find it. Okay, let's start with the storage level. That's the logical place.'

Shea chuckled. 'The logical place is usually the worst place to look.' But they all headed for the power-ramp once more and the additional flight upward.

The storage level had a musty, unused odor to it. Moore turned on the precipitron. 'I don't think we've precipitated the dust in two years. That shows you how often I'm up here. Now, let's see; if it's anywhere at all, it would be in with the bachelor collection; I mean the junk I've been hanging on to since bachelor days. We can start here.'

Moore started leafing through the contents of plastic collapsibles while Brandon kept peering anxiously over his shoulder.

Moore said, 'What do you know? My college yearbook. I was a sonist in those days; a real bug on it. In fact, I managed to get a voice recording with the picture of every senior in this book.' He tapped its cover fondly. 'You could swear there was nothing there but the usual trimensional photos, but each one has an imprisoned —'

He grew aware of Brandon's frown and said, 'Okay. I'll keep looking.'

He gave up on the collapsibles and opened a trunk of heavy, old-fashioned woodite. He separated the contents of the various compartments.

Brandon said, 'Hey, is that it?'

He pointed to a small cylinder that rolled out on the floor with a small clunk.

Moore said, 'I don't — Yes! That's the pen. There it is. And here's the field-glass. Neither one works, of course. They're both broken. At least I suppose the pen's broken. Something's loose and rattles in it. Hear? I wouldn't have the slightest idea as to how to fill it so I can check as to whether it really works. They haven't even made ink-spray cartridges in years.'

Brandon held it under the light. 'It has initials on it.'

'Oh? I don't remember noticing any.'

'It's pretty worn down. It looks like J.K.Q.'

'Q?'

'Right, and that's an unusual letter with which to start a last name. This pen might have belonged to Quentin; an heirloom he kept for luck or sentiment. It might have belonged to a great-grandfather in the days when they used pens like this; a great-grandfather called Jason Knight Quentin or Judah Kent Quentin or something like that. We can check the names of Quentin's ancestors through Multivac.'

Moore nodded. 'I think maybe we should. See, you've got

123

me as crazy as you are.'

'And if this is so, it proves you picked it up in Quentin's room, so you picked up the field-glass there, too.'

'Now hold it. I don't remember that I picked them both up in the same place. I don't remember the scrounging over the outside of the wreck that well.'

Brandon turned the small field-glass over and over under the light. 'No initials here.'

'Did you expect any?'

'I don't see anything in fact, except this narrow joining mark here.' He ran his thumbnail into the fine groove that circled the glass near its thicker end. He tried to twist it unsuccessfully. 'One piece.' He put it to his eye. 'This thing doesn't work.'

'I told you it was broken. No lenses.'

Shea broke in. 'You've got to expect a little damage when a spaceship hits a good-sized meteor and goes to pieces.'

'So even if this were it,' said Moore, pessimistic again, 'if this were the optikon, it would not do us any good.'

He took the field-glass from Brandon and felt along the empty rims. 'You can't even tell where the lenses belonged. There's no groove I can feel into which they might have been seated. It's as if there never – *Hey!*' He exploded the syllable violently.

'Hey what?' said Brandon.

'The name! The name of the thing!'

'Optikon, you mean?'

'Optikon, I don't mean! Fitzimmons, on the tube, called it an optikon and we thought he said "an – optikon".'

'Well, he did,' said Brandon.

'Sure,' said Shea. 'I heard him.'

'You just thought you heard him. He said "anoptikon". – Don't you get it? Not "an optikon", two words, "anopti-kon", one word.'

'Oh,' said Brandon, blankly. 'And what's the difference.'

'A hell of a difference. "An optikon" would mean an instrument with lenses, but "anoptikon", one word, has the Greek prefix "an-" which means "no". Words of Greek derivation use it for "no". Anarchy means "no government", anemia means "no blood", anonymous means "no name"

124

and anoptikon means —'

'No lenses,' cried Brandon.

'Right! Quentin must have been working on an optical device without lenses and this may be it and it may not be broken.'

Shea said, 'But you don't see anything when you look through it.'

'It must be set to neutral,' said Moore. 'There must be some way of adjusting it.' Like Brandon, he placed it in both hands and tried to twist it about that circumscribing groove. He placed pressure on it, grunting.

'Don't break it,' said Brandon.

'It's giving. Either it's supposed to be stiff or else it's corroded shut.' He stopped, looked at the instrument impatiently and put it to his eye again. He whirled, unpolarized a window and looked out at the lights of the city.

'I'll be dumped in Space,' he breathed.

Brandon said, 'What? What?'

Moore handed the instrument to Brandon wordlessly. Brandon put it to his eyes and cried out sharply, 'It's a telescope.'

Shea said at once, 'Let me see.'

They spent nearly an hour with it, converting it into a telescope with turns in one direction, a microscope with turns in the other.

'How does it work?' Brandon kept asking.

'I don't know,' Moore kept saying. In the end, he said, 'I'm sure it involves concentrated force-fields. We are turning against considerable field resistance. With large instruments, power-adjustment will be required.'

'It's a pretty cute trick,' said Shea.

'It's more than that,' said Moore. 'I'll bet it represents a completely new turn in theoretical physics. It focuses light without lenses, and it can be adjusted to gather light over a wider and wider area without any change in focal length. I'll bet we could duplicate the five-hundred-inch Ceres telescope in one direction and an electron miscroscope in the other. What's more I don't see any chromatic aberration, so it must bend light of all wave-lengths equally. Maybe it bends radio waves and gamma rays also. Maybe it distorts

125

gravity, if gravity is some kind of radiation. Maybe —'

'Worth money?' asked Shea, breaking in dryly.

'All kinds if someone can figure out how it works.'

'Then we don't go to Trans-space Insurance with this. We go to a lawyer first. Did we sign these things away with our salvage rights or didn't we? You had them already in your possession before signing the paper. For that matter, is the paper any good if we didn't know what we were signing away? Maybe it might be considered fraud.'

'As a matter of fact,' said Moore, 'with something like this, I don't know if any private company ought to own it. We ought to check with some Government agency. If there's money in it —'

But Brandon was pounding both fists on his knees. 'To *hell* with the money, Warren. I mean I'll take any money that comes my way but that's not the important thing. We're going to be famous, man, famous! Imagine the story. A fabulous treasure lost in space. A giant corporation combing space for twenty years to find it and all the time we, the forgotten ones, have it in our possession. Then, on the twentieth anniversary of the original loss, we find it again. If this thing works; if anoptics becomes a great new scientific technique, they'll *never* forget us.'

Moore grinned, then started laughing. 'That's right. You did it, Mark. You did just what you set out to do. You've rescued us from being marooned in oblivion.'

'We all did it,' said Brandon. 'Mike Shea started us off with the necessary basic information. I worked out the theory, and you had the instrument.'

'Okay. It's late, and the wife will be back soon, so let's get the ball rolling right away. Multivac will tell us which agency would be appropriate and who —'

'No, no,' said Brandon. 'Ritual first. The closing toast of the anniversary, please, and with the appropriate change. Won't you oblige, Warren?' He passed over the still half-full bottle of *Jabra* water.

Carefully, Moore filled each small glass precisely to the brim. 'Gentlemen,' he said solemnly, 'a toast.' The three raised the glasses in unison. 'Gentlemen, I give you the *Silver Queen* souvenirs *we used to have*.'

126

THE BILLIARD BALL

JAMES PRISS – I suppose I ought to say Professor James Priss, though everyone is sure to know whom I mean even without the title – always spoke slowly.

I know. I interviewed him often enough. He had the greatest mind since Einstein, but it didn't work quickly. He admitted his slowness often. Maybe it was *because* he had so great a mind that it didn't work quickly.

He would say something in slow abstraction, then he would think, and then he would say something more. Even over trivial matters, his giant mind would hover uncertainly, adding a touch here and then another there.

Would the Sun rise tomorrow, I can imagine him wondering. What do we mean by 'rise'? Can we be certain that tomorrow will come? Is the term 'Sun' completely unambiguous in this connection?

Add to this habit of speech a bland countenance, rather pale, with no expression except for a general look of uncertainty; gray hair, rather thin, neatly combed; business suits of an invariably conservative cut; and you have what Professor James Priss was – a retiring person, completely lacking in magnetism.

That's why nobody in the world, except myself, could possibly suspect him of being a murderer. And even I am not sure. After all, he *was* slow-thinking; he was *always* slow-thinking. Is it conceivable that at one crucial moment he managed to think quickly and act at once?

It doesn't matter. Even if he murdered, he got away with it. It is far too late now to try to reverse matters and I wouldn't succeed in doing so even if I decided to let this be published.

Edward Bloom was Priss's classmate in college, and an associate, through circumstance, for a generation afterward. They were equal in age and in their propensity for the bachelor life, but opposites in everything else that mattered.

Bloom was a living flash of light; colorful, tall, broad, loud, brash, and self-confident. He had a mind that resembled a meteor strike in the sudden and unexpected way it could seize the essential. He was no theoretician, as Priss was; Bloom had neither the patience for it, nor the capacity to concentrate intense thought upon a single abstract point. He admitted that; he boasted of it.

What he did have was an uncanny way of seeing the application of a theory; of seeing the manner in which it could be put to use. In the cold marble block of abstract structure, he could see, without apparent difficulty, the intricate design of a marvelous device. The block would fall apart at his touch and leave the device.

It is a well-known story, and not too badly exaggerated, that nothing Bloom ever built had failed to work, or to be patentable, or to be profitable. By the time he was forty-five, he was one of the richest men on Earth.

And if Bloom the Technician were adapted to one particular matter more than anything else, it was to the way of thought of Priss the Theoretician. Bloom's greatest gadgets were built upon Priss's greatest thoughts, and as Bloom grew wealthy and famous, Priss gained phenomenal respect among his colleagues.

Naturally it was to be expected that when Priss advanced his Two-Field Theory, Bloom would set about at once to build the first practical anti-gravity device.

My job was to find human interest in the Two-Field Theory for the subscribers to *Tele-News Press*, and you get that by trying to deal with human beings and not with abstract ideas. Since my interviewee was Professor Priss, that wasn't easy.

Naturally, I was going to ask about the possibilities of anti-gravity, which interested everyone; and not about the Two-Field Theory, which no one could understand.

'Anti-gravity?' Priss compressed his pale lips and considered. 'I'm not entirely sure that it is possible, or ever will be. I haven't – uh – worked the matter out to my satisfaction. I don't entirely see whether the Two-Field equations would have a finite solution, which they would have to have, of course, if —' And then he went off into a brown study.

I prodded him. 'Bloom says he thinks such a device can be built.'

Priss nodded. 'Well, yes, but I wonder. Ed Bloom has had an amazing knack at seeing the unobvious in the past. He has an unusual mind. It's certainly made him rich enough.'

We were sitting in Priss's apartment. Ordinary middle-class. I couldn't help a quick glance this way and that. Priss was not wealthy.

I don't think he read my mind. He saw me look. And I think it was on *his* mind. He said, 'Wealth isn't the usual reward for the pure scientist. Or even a particularly desirable one.'

Maybe so, at that, I thought. Priss certainly had his own kind of reward. He was the third person in history to win two Nobel Prizes, and the first to have both of them in the sciences and both of them unshared. You can't complain about that. And if he wasn't rich, neither was he poor.

But he didn't sound like a contented man. Maybe it wasn't Bloom's wealth alone that irked Priss; maybe it was Bloom's fame among the people of Earth generally; maybe it was the fact that Bloom was a celebrity wherever he went, whereas Priss, outside scientific conventions and faculty clubs, was largely anonymous.

I can't say how much of all this was in my eyes or in the way I wrinkled the creases in my forehead, but Priss went on to say, 'But we're friends, you know. We play billiards once or twice a week. I beat him regularly.'

(I never published that statement. I checked it with Bloom, who made a long counterstatement that began: 'He beats *me* at billiards. That jackass —' and grew increasingly personal thereafter. As a matter of fact, neither one was a novice at billiards. I watched them play once for a short while, after the statement and counterstatement, and both handled the cue with professional aplomb. What's more, both played for blood, and there was no friendship in the game that I could see.)

I said, 'Would you care to predict whether Bloom will manage to build an anti-gravity device?'

'You mean would I commit myself to anything? Hmm. Well, let's consider, young man. Just what do we mean by anti-gravity? Our conception of gravity is built around Einstein's General Theory of Relativity, which is now a century and a half old but which, within its limits, remains firm. We can picture it —'

I listened politely. I'd heard Priss on the subject before, but if I was to get anything out of him – which wasn't certain – I'd have to let him work his way through in his own way.

'We can picture it,' he said, 'by imagining the Universe to be a flat, thin, superflexible sheet of untearable rubber. If we picture mass as being associated with weight, as it is on the surface of the Earth, then we would expect a mass, resting upon the rubber sheet, to make an indentation. The greater the mass, the deeper the indentation.

'In the actual Universe,' he went on, 'all sorts of masses exist, and so our rubber sheet must be pictured as riddled with indentations. Any object rolling along the sheet would dip into and out of the indentations it passed, veering and changing direction as it did so. It is this veer and change of direction that we interpret as demonstrating the existence of a force of gravity. If the moving object comes close enough to the center of the indentation and is moving slowly enough, it gets trapped and whirls round and round that indentation. In the absence of friction, it keeps up that whirl forever. In other words, what Isaac Newton interpreted as a force, Albert Einstein interpreted as geometrical distortion.'

He paused at this point. He had been speaking fairly fluently – for him – since he was saying something he had said often before. But now he began to pick his way.

He said, 'So in trying to produce anti-gravity, we are trying to alter the geometry of the Universe. If we carry on our metaphor, we are trying to straighten out the indented rubber sheet. We could imagine ourselves getting under the indenting mass and lifting it upward, supporting it so as to prevent it from making an indentation. If we make the

130

rubber sheet flat in that way, then we create a Universe – or at least a portion of the Universe – in which gravity doesn't exist. A rolling body would pass the non-indenting mass without altering its direction of travel a bit, and we could interpret this as meaning that the mass was exerting no gravitational force. In order to accomplish this feat, however, we need a mass equivalent to the indenting mass. To produce anti-gravity on Earth in this way, we would have to make use of a mass equal to that of Earth and poise it above our heads, so to speak.'

I interrupted him. 'But your Two-Field Theory —'

'Exactly. General Relativity does not explain both the gravitational field and the electromagnetic field in a single set of equations. Einstein spent half his life searching for that single set – for a Unified Field Theory – and failed. All who followed Einstein also failed. I, however, began with the assumption that there were two fields that could not be unified and followed the consequences, which I can explain, in part, in terms of the "rubber sheet" metaphor.'

Now we came to something I wasn't sure I had ever heard before. 'How does that go?' I asked.

'Suppose that, instead of trying to lift the indenting mass, we try to stiffen the sheet itself, make it less indentable. It would contract, at least over a small area, and become flatter. Gravity would weaken, and so would mass, for the two are essentially the same phenomenon in terms of the indented Universe. If we could make the rubber sheet completely flat, both gravity and mass would disappear altogether.

'Under the proper conditions, the electromagnetic field could be made to counter the gravitational field, and serve to stiffen the indented fabric of the Universe. The electromagnetic field is tremendously stronger than the gravitational field, so the former could be made to overcome the latter.'

I said uncertainly, 'But you say "under the proper conditions". Can those proper conditions you speak of be achieved, Professor?'

'That is what I don't know,' said Priss thoughtfully and slowly. 'If the Universe were really a rubber sheet, its stiffness would have to reach an infinite value before it could be expected to remain completely flat under an indenting mass. If that is also so in the real Universe, then an infinitely intense electromagnetic field would be required and that would mean anti-gravity would be impossible.'

'But Bloom says —'

'Yes, I imagine Bloom thinks a finite field will do, if it can be properly applied. Still, however ingenious he is,' and Priss smiled narrowly, 'we needn't take him to be infallible. His grasp on theory is quite faulty. He – he never earned his college degree, did you know that?'

I was about to say that I knew that. After all, everyone did. But there was a touch of eagerness in Priss's voice as he said it and I looked up in time to catch animation in his eye, as though he were delighted to spread that piece of news. So I nodded my head as if I were filing it for future reference.

'Then you would say, Professor Priss,' I prodded again, 'that Bloom is probably wrong and that anti-gravity is impossible?'

And finally Priss nodded and said, 'The gravitational field can be weakened, of course, but if by anti-gravity we mean a true zero-gravity field – no gravity at all over a significant volume of space – then I suspect anti-gravity may turn out to be impossible, despite Bloom.'

And I had, after a fashion, what I wanted.

I wasn't able to see Bloom for nearly three months after that, and when I did see him he was in an angry mood.

He had grown angry at once, of course, when the news first broke concerning Priss's statement. He let it be known that Priss would be invited to the eventual display of the anti-gravity device as soon as it was constructed, and would even be asked to participate in the demonstration. Some reporter – not I, unfortunately – caught him between appointments and asked him to elaborate on that and he said:

'I'll have the device eventually; soon, maybe. And you can be there, and so can anyone else the press would care to have there. And Professor James Priss can be there. He can represent Theoretical Science and after I have demonstrated anti-gravity, he can adjust his theory to explain it. I'm sure he will know how to make his adjustments in masterly fashion and show exactly why I couldn't possibly have failed. He might do it now and save time, but I suppose he won't.'

It was all said very politely, but you could hear the snarl under the rapid flow of words.

Yet he continued his occasional game of billiards with Priss and when the two met they behaved with complete propriety. One could tell the progress Bloom was making by their respective attitudes to the press. Bloom grew curt and even snappish, while Priss developed an increasing good humor.

When my umpteenth request for an interview with Bloom was finally accepted, I wondered if perhaps that meant a break in Bloom's quest. I had a little daydream of him announcing final success to *me*.

It didn't work out that way. He met me in his office at Bloom Enterprises in upstate New York. It was a wonderful setting, well away from any populated area, elaborately landscaped, and covering as much ground as a rather large industrial establishment. Edison at his height, two centuries ago, had never been as phenomenally successful as Bloom.

But Bloom was not in a good humor. He came striding in ten minutes late and went snarling past his secretary's desk with the barest nod in my direction. He was wearing a lab coat, unbuttoned.

He threw himself into his chair and said, 'I'm sorry if I've kept you waiting, but I didn't have as much time as I had hoped.' Bloom was a born showman and knew better than to antagonize the press, but I had the feeling he was having a great deal of difficulty at that moment in adhering to this principle.

I made the obvious guess. 'I am given to understand, sir, that your recent tests have been unsuccessful.'

'Who told you that?'

'I would say it was general knowledge, Mr. Bloom.'

'No, it isn't. Don't say that, young man. There is no general knowledge about what goes on in my laboratories and workshops. You're stating the Professor's opinions, aren't you? Priss's, I mean.'

133

'No, I'm —'

'Of course you are. Aren't you the one to whom he made that statement – that anti-gravity is impossible?'

'He didn't make the statement that flatly.'

'He never says anything flatly, but it was flat enough for him, and not as flat as I'll have his damned rubber-sheet Universe before I'm finished.'

'Then does that mean you're making progress, Mr. Bloom.'

'You know I am,' he said with a snap. 'Or you should know. Weren't you at the demonstration last week?'

'Yes, I was.'

I judged Bloom to be in trouble or he wouldn't be mentioning that demonstration. It worked but it was not a world beater. Between the two poles of a magnet a region of lessened gravity was produced.

It was done very cleverly. A Mössbauer-Effect Balance was used to probe the space between the poles. If you've never seen an M-E Balance in action, it consists primarily of a tight monochromatic beam of gamma rays shot down the low-gravity field. The gamma rays change wavelength slightly but measurably under the influence of the gravitational field and if anything happens to alter the intensity of the field, the wavelength-change shifts correspondingly. It is an extremely delicate method for probing a gravitational field and it worked like a charm. There was no question but that Bloom had lowered gravity.

The trouble was that it had been done before by others. Bloom, to be sure, had made use of circuits that greatly increased the ease with which such an effect had been achieved – his system was typically ingenious and had been duly patented – and he maintained that it was by this method that anti-gravity would become not merely a scientific curiosity but a practical affair with industrial applications.

Perhaps. But it was an incomplete job and he didn't usually make a fuss over incompleteness. He wouldn't have done so this time if he weren't desperate to display *something*.

I said, 'It's my impression that what you accomplished at

that preliminary demonstration was 0·82 g, and better than that was achieved in Brazil last spring.'

'That so? Well, calculate the energy input in Brazil and here, and then tell me the difference in gravity decrease per kilowatt-hour. You'll be surprised.'

'But the point is, can you reach 0 g – zero gravity? That's what Professor Priss thinks may be impossible. Everyone agrees that merely lessening the intensity of the field is no great feat.'

Bloom's fist clenched. I had the feeling that a key experiment had gone wrong that day and he was annoyed almost past endurance. Bloom hated to be balked by the Universe.

He said, 'Theoreticians make me sick.' He said it in a low, controlled voice, as though he were finally tired of not saying it, and he was going to speak his mind and be damned. 'Priss has won two Nobel Prizes for sloshing around a few equations, but what has he done with it? Nothing! I *have* done something with it and I'm going to do more with it, whether Priss likes it or not.

'*I*'m the one people will remember. *I*'m the one who gets the credit. He can keep his damned title and his Prizes and his kudos from the scholars. Listen, I'll tell you what gripes him. Plain old-fashioned jealousy. It kills him that I get what I get for doing. He wants it for *thinking*.

'I said to him once – we play billiards together, you know —'

It was at this point that I quoted Priss's statement about billiards and got Bloom's counterstatement. I never published either. That was just trivia.

'We play billiards,' said Bloom, when he had cooled down, 'and I've won my share of games. We keep things friendly enough. What the hell – college chums and all that – though how he got through, I'll never know. He made it in physics, of course, and in math, but he got a bare pass – out of pity, I think – in every humanities course he ever took.'

'You did not get your degree, did you, Mr. Bloom?' That was sheer mischief on my part. I was enjoying his eruption.

'I quit to go into business, damn it. My academic average, over the three years I attended, was a strong B. Don't imagine anything else, you hear? Hell, by the time Priss got his Ph D., I was working on my second million.'

He went on, clearly irritated. 'Anyway, we were playing billiards and I said to him, 'Jim, the average man will never understand why you get the Nobel Prize when I'm the one who gets the results. Why do you need two? Give me one!' He stood there, chalking up his cue, and then he said in his soft namby-pamby way, "You have two billions, Ed. Give me one." So you see, he wants the money.'

I said, 'I take it you don't mind his getting the honor?'

For a minute I thought he was going to order me out, but he didn't. He laughed instead, waved his hand in front of him, as though he were erasing something from an invisible blackboard in front of him. He said, 'Oh well, forget it. All that is off the record. Listen, do you want a statement? Okay. Things didn't go right today and I blew my top a bit, but it will clear up. I think I know what's wrong. And if I don't, I'm going to know.

'Look, you can say that *I* say that we *don't* need infinite electromagnetic intensity; we *will* flatten out the rubber sheet; we *will* have zero gravity. And when we get it, I'll have the damndest demonstration you ever saw, exclusively for the press and for Priss, and you'll be invited. And you can say it won't be long. Okay?'

Okay!

I had time after that to see each man once or twice more. I even saw them together when I was present at one of their billiard games. As I said before, both of them were *good*.

But the call to the demonstration did not come as quickly as all that. It arrived six weeks less than a year after Bloom gave me his statement. And at that, perhaps it was unfair to expect quicker work.

I had a special engraved invitation, with the assurance of a cocktail hour first. Bloom never did things by halves and he was planning to have a pleased and satisfied group of reporters on hand. There was an arrangement for trimensional TV, too. Bloom felt completely confident, obviously; confident enough to be willing to trust the demonstration in every living room on the planet.

I called up Professor Priss, to make sure he was invited too. He was.

'Do you plan to attend, sir?'

There was a pause and the professor's face on the screen was a study in uncertain reluctance. 'A demonstration of this sort is most unsuitable where a serious scientific matter is in question. I do not like to encourage such things.'

I was afraid he would beg off, and the dramatics of the situation would be greatly lessened if he were not there. But then, perhaps, he decided he dared not play the chicken before the world. With obvious distaste he said, 'Of course, Ed Bloom is not really a scientist and he must have his day in the sun. I'll be there.'

'Do you think Mr. Bloom can produce zero gravity, sir?'

'Uh ... Mr. Bloom sent me a copy of the design of his device and ... and I'm not certain. Perhaps he can do it, if ... uh ... he says he can do it. Of course' – he paused again for quite a long time – 'I think I would like to see it.'

So would I, and so would many others.

The staging was impeccable. A whole floor of the main building at Bloom Enterprises – the one on the hilltop – was cleared. There were the promised cocktails and a splendid array of hors d'oeuvres, soft music and lighting, and a carefully dressed and thoroughly jovial Edward Bloom playing the perfect host, while a number of polite and unobtrusive menials fetched and carried. All was geniality and amazing confidence.

James Priss was late and I caught Bloom watching the corners of the crowd and beginning to grow a little grim about the edges. Then Priss arrived, dragging a volume of colorlessness in with him, a drabness that was unaffected by the noise and the absolute splendor (no other word would describe it – or else it was the two martinis glowing inside me) that filled the room.

Bloom saw him and his face was illuminated at once. He bounced across the floor, seized the smaller man's hand and dragged him to the bar.

'Jim! Glad to see you! What'll you have? Hell, man, I'd have called it off if you hadn't showed. Can't have this thing without the star, you know.' He wrung Priss's hand. 'It's your theory, you know. We poor mortals can't do a thing without you few, you damned *few* few, pointing the way.'

He was being ebullient, handing out the flattery, because he could afford to do so now. He was fattening Priss for the kill.

Priss tried to refuse a drink, with some sort of mutter, but a glass was pressed into his hand and Bloom raised his voice to a bull roar.

'Gentlemen! A moment's quiet, please. To Professor Priss, the greatest mind since Einstein, two-time Nobel Laureate, father of the Two-Field Theory, and inspirer of the demonstration we are about to see — even if he didn't think it would work, and had the guts to say so publicly.'

There was a distinct titter of laughter that quickly faded out and Priss looked as grim as his face could manage.

'But now that Professor Priss is here,' said Bloom, 'and we've had our toast, let's get on with it. Follow me, gentlemen!'

The demonstration was in a much more elaborate place than had housed the earlier one. This time it was on the top floor of the building. Different magnets were involved — smaller ones, by heaven — but as nearly as I could tell, the same M-E Balance was in place.

One thing was new, however, and it staggered everybody, drawing much more attention than anything else in the room. It was a billiard table, resting under one pole of the magnet. Beneath it was the companion pole. A round hole, about a foot across, was stamped out of the very center of the table and it was obvious that the zero-gravity field, if it was to be produced, would be produced through that hole in the center of the billiard table.

It was as though the whole demonstration had been designed, surrealist fashion, to point out the victory of Bloom over Priss. This was to be another version of their everlasting billiards competition and Bloom was going to win.

I don't know if the other newsmen took matters in that fashion, but I think Priss did. I turned to look at him and saw that he was still holding the drink that had been forced into his hand. He rarely drank, I knew, but now he lifted the glass to his lips and emptied it in two swallows. He stared at that billiard ball and I needed no gift of ESP to realize that he took it as a deliberate snap of fingers under his nose.

Bloom led us to the twenty seats that surrounded three sides of the table, leaving the fourth free as a working area. Priss was carefully escorted to the seat commanding the most convenient view. Priss glanced quickly at the trimensional cameras which were now working. I wondered if he were thinking of leaving but deciding that he couldn't in the full glare of the eyes of the world.

Essentially, the demonstration was simple; it was the production that counted. There were dials in plain view that measured the energy expenditure. There were others that transferred the M-E Balance readings into a position and a size that were visible to all. Everything was arranged for easy trimensional viewing.

Bloom explained each step in a genial way, with one or two pauses in which he turned to Priss for a confirmation that had to come. He didn't do it often enough to make it obvious, but just enough to turn Priss upon the spit of his own torment. From where I sat I could look across the table and see Priss on the other side.

He had the look of a man in Hell.

As we all know, Bloom succeeded. The M-E Balance showed the gravitational intensity to be sinking steadily as the electro-magnetic field was intensified. There were cheers when it dropped below the 0·52 g mark. A red line indicated that on the dial.

'The 0·52 g mark, as you know,' said Bloom confidently, 'represents the previous record low in gravitational intensity. We are now lower than that at a cost in electricity that is less than ten per cent what it cost at the time that mark was set. And we will go lower still.'

Bloom – I think deliberately, for the sake of the suspense – slowed the drop toward the end, letting the trimensional cameras switch back and forth between the gap in the billiard table and the dial on which the M-E Balance reading was lowering.

Bloom said suddenly, 'Gentlemen, you will find dark

goggles in the pouch on the side of each chair. Please put them on now. The zero-gravity field will soon be established and it will radiate a light rich in ultraviolet.'

He put goggles on himself, and there was a momentary rustle as others went on too.

I think no one breathed during the last minute, when the dial reading dropped to zero and held fast. And just as that happened a cylinder of light sprang into existence from pole to pole through the hole in the billiard table.

There was a ghost of twenty sighs at that. Someone called out, 'Mr. Bloom, what is the reason for the light?'

'It's characteristic of the zero-gravity field,' said Bloom smoothly, which was no answer, of course.

Reporters were standing up now, crowding about the edge of the table. Bloom waved them back. 'Please, gentlemen, stand clear!'

Only Priss remained sitting. He seemed lost in thought and I have been certain ever since that it was the goggles that obscured the possible significance of everything that followed. I didn't see his eyes. I couldn't. And that meant neither I nor anyone else could even begin to make a guess as to what was going on behind those eyes. Well, maybe we couldn't have made such a guess, even if the goggles hadn't been there, but who can say?

Bloom was raising his voice again. 'Please! The demonstration is not yet over. So far, we've only repeated what I have done before. I have now produced a zero-gravity field and I have shown it can be done practically. But I want to demonstrate something of what such a field can do. What we are going to see next will be something that has never been seen, not even by myself. I have not experimented in this direction, much as I would have liked to, because I have felt that Professor Priss deserved the honor of —'

Priss looked up sharply. 'What – what —'

'Professor Priss,' said Bloom, smiling broadly, 'I would like you to perform the first experiment involving the inter-action of a solid object with a zero-gravity field. Notice that the field has been formed in the center of a billiard table. The world knows your phenomenal skill in billiards, Pro-fessor, a talent second only to your amazing aptitude in

140

theoretical physics. Won't you send a billiard ball into the zero-gravity volume?'·

Eagerly he was handing a ball and cue to the professor. Priss, his eyes hidden by the goggles, stared at them and only very slowly, very uncertainly, reached out to take them.

I wonder what his eyes were showing. I wonder, too, how much of the decision to have Priss play billiards at the demonstration was due to Bloom's anger at Priss's remark about their periodic game, the remark I had quoted. Had I been, in my way, responsible for what followed?

'Come, stand up, Professor,' said Bloom, 'and let me have your seat. The show is yours from now on. Go ahead!'

Bloom seated himself, and still talked, in a voice that grew more organlike with each moment. 'Once Professor Priss sends the ball into the volume of zero gravity, it will no longer be affected by Earth's gravitational field. It will remain truly motionless while the Earth rotates about its axis and travels about the Sun. In this latitude, and at this time of day, I have calculated that the Earth, in its motions, will sink downward. We will move with it and the ball will stand still. To us it will seem to rise up and away from the Earth's surface. Watch.'

Priss seemed to stand in front of the table in frozen paralysis. Was it surprise? Astonishment? I don't know. I'll never know. Did he make a move to interrupt Bloom's little speech, or was he just suffering from an agonized reluctance to play the ignominious part into which he was being forced by his adversary?

Priss turned to the billiard table, looking first at it, then back at Bloom. Every reporter was on his feet, crowding as closely as possible in order to get a good view. Only Bloom himself remained seated, smiling and isolated. He, of course, was not watching the table, or the ball, or the zero-gravity field. As nearly as I could tell through the goggles, he was watching Priss.

Priss turned to the table and placed his ball. He was going to be the agent that was to bring final and dramatic triumph to Bloom and make himself – the man who said it couldn't be done – the goat to be mocked forever.

Perhaps he felt there was no way out. Or perhaps —

With a sure stroke of his cue, he set the ball into motion. It was not going quickly, and every eye followed it. It struck the side of the table and caromed. It was going even slower now as though Priss himself were increasing the suspense and making Bloom's triumph the more dramatic.

I had a perfect view, for I was standing on the side of the table opposite from that where Priss was. I could see the ball moving toward the glitter of the zero-gravity field and beyond it I could see those portions of the seated Bloom which were not hidden by that glitter.

The ball approached the zero-gravity volume, seemed to hang on the edge for a moment, and then was gone, with a streak of light, the sound of a thunderclap and the sudden smell of burning cloth.

We yelled. We all yelled.

I've seen the scene on television since – along with the rest of the world. I can see myself in the film during that fifteen-second period of wild confusion, but I don't really recognize my face.

Fifteen seconds!

And then we discovered Bloom. He was still sitting in the chair, his arms still folded, but there was a hole the size of a billiard ball through forearm, chest, and back. The better part of his heart, as it later turned out under autopsy, had been neatly punched out.

They turned off the device. They called in the police. They dragged off Priss, who was in a state of utter collapse. I wasn't much better off, to tell the truth, and if any reporter then on the scene ever tried to say he remained a cool observer of that scene, then he's a cool liar.

It was some months before I got to see Priss again. He had lost some weight but seemed well otherwise. Indeed, there was color in his cheeks and an air of decision about him. He was better dressed than I had ever seen him to be.

He said, 'I know what happened *now*. If I had had time to think, I would have known then. But I am a slow thinker, and poor Ed Bloom was so intent on running a great show and doing it so well that he carried me along with him.

Naturally, I've been trying to make up for some of the damage I unwittingly caused.'

'You can't bring Bloom back to life,' I said soberly.

'No, I can't,' he said, just as soberly. 'But there's Bloom Enterprises to think of, too. What happened at the demonstration, in full view of the world, was the worst possible advertisement for zero gravity, and it's important that the story be made clear. That is why *I* have asked to see *you*.'

'Yes?'

'If I had been a quicker thinker, I would have known Ed was speaking the purest nonsense when he said that the billiard ball would slowly rise in the zero-gravity field. It *couldn't* be so! If Bloom hadn't despised theory so, if he hadn't been so intent on being proud of his own ignorance of theory, he'd have known it himself.

'The Earth's motion, after all, isn't the only motion involved, young man. The Sun itself moves in a vast orbit about the center of the Milky Way Galaxy. And the Galaxy moves too, in some not very clearly defined way. If the billiard ball were subjected to zero gravity, you might think of it as being unaffected by any of these motions and therefore of suddenly falling into a state of absolute rest – when there is no such thing as absolute rest.'

Priss shook his head slowly. 'The trouble with Ed, I think, was that he was thinking of the kind of zero gravity one gets in a spaceship in free fall, when people float in mid-air. He expected the ball to float in mid-air. However, in a spaceship, zero gravity is not the result of an absence of gravitation, but merely the result of two objects, a ship and a man within the ship, falling at the same rate, responding to gravity in precisely the same way, so that each is motionless with respect to the other.

'In the zero-gravity field produced by Ed, there was a flattening of the rubber-sheet Universe, which means an actual loss of mass. Everything in that field, including molecules of air caught within it, and the billiard ball I pushed into it, was completely massless as long as it remained with it. A completely massless object can move in only one way.'

He paused, inviting the question. I asked, 'What motion

143

would that be?'

'Motion at the speed of light. Any massless object, such as a neutrino or a photon, must travel at the speed of light as long as it exists. In fact, light moves at that speed only because it is made up of photons. As soon as the billiard ball entered the zero-gravity field and lost its mass, it too assumed the speed of light at once and left.'

I shook my head. 'But didn't it regain its mass as soon as it left the zero-gravity volume?'

'It certainly did, and at once it began to be affected by the gravitational field and to slow up in response to the friction of the air and the top of the billiard table. But imagine how much friction it would take to slow up an object the mass of a billiard ball going at the speed of light. It went through the hundred-mile thickness of our atmosphere in a thousandth of a second and I doubt that it was slowed more than a few miles a second in doing so, a few miles out of 186,282 of them. On the way, it scorched the top of the billiard table, broke cleanly through the edge, went through poor Ed and the window too, punching out neat circles because it had passed through before the neighboring portions of something even as brittle as glass had a chance to split and splinter.

'It is extremely fortunate we were on the top floor of a building set in a countrified area. If we were in the city, it might have passed through a number of buildings and killed a number of people. By now that billiard ball is off in space, far beyond the edge of the Solar System and it will continue to travel so forever, at nearly the speed of light, until it happens to strike an object large enough to stop it. And then it will gouge out a sizeable crater.'

I played with the notion and was not sure I liked it. 'How is that possible? The billiard ball entered the zero-gravity volume almost at a standstill. I saw it. And you say it left with an incredible quantity of kinetic energy. Where did the energy come from?'

Priss shrugged. 'It came from nowhere! the law of conservation of energy only holds under the conditions in which general relativity is valid; that is, in an indented-rubber-sheet universe. Wherever the indentation is flattened out, general relativity no longer holds, and energy can be created and destroyed freely. That accounts for the radiation along the cylindrical surface of the zero-gravity volume. That radiation, you remember, Bloom did not explain, and, I fear, could not explain. If he had only experimented further first; if he had only not been so foolishly anxious to put on his show —'

'What accounts for the radiation, sir?'

'The molecules of air inside the volume. Each assumes the speed of light and comes smashing outward. They're only molecules, not billiard balls, so they're stopped, but the kinetic energy of their motion is converted into energetic radiation. It's continuous because new molecules are always drifting in, and attaining the speed of light and smashing out.'

'Then energy is being created continuously?'

'Exactly. And that is what we must make clear to the public. Anti-gravity is not primarily a device to lift spaceships or to revolutionize mechanical movement. Rather, it is the source of an endless supply of free energy, since part of the energy produced can be diverted to maintain the field that keeps that portion of the Universe flat. What Ed Bloom invented, without knowing it, was not just anti-gravity, but the first successful perpetual-motion machine of the first class – one that manufactures energy out of nothing.'

I said slowly, 'Any one of us could have been killed by that billiard ball, is that right, Professor? It might have come out in any direction.'

Priss said, 'Well, massless photons emerge from any light source at the speed of light in any direction; that's why a candle casts light in all directions. The massless air molecules come out of the zero-gravity volume in all directions, which is why the entire cylinder radiates. But the billiard ball was only one object. It could have come out in any direction, but it had to come out in some one direction, chosen at random, and the chosen direction happened to be the one that caught Ed.'

That was it. Everyone knows the consequences. Mankind had free energy and so we have the world we have now. Professor Priss was placed in charge of its development by the board of Bloom Enterprises, and in time he was as rich and famous as ever Edward Bloom had been. And Priss still has two Nobel Prizes in addition.

Only ...

I keep thinking. Photons smash out from a light source in all directions because they are created at the moment and there is no reason for them to move in one direction more than in another. Air molecules come out of a zero-gravity field in all directions because they enter it in all directions.

But what about a single billiard ball, entering a zero-gravity field from one particular direction? Does it come out in the same direction or in any direction?

I've inquired delicately, but theoretical physicists don't seem to be sure, and I can find no record that Bloom Enterprises, which is the only organization working with zero-gravity fields, has ever experimented in the matter. Someone at the organization once told me that the uncertainty principle guarantees the random emersion of an object entering in any direction. But then why don't they try the experiment?

Could it be, then ...

Could it be that for once Priss's mind had been working quickly? Could it be that, under the pressure of what Bloom was trying to do to him, Priss had suddenly seen everything? He had been studying the radiation surrounding the zero-gravity volume. He might have realized its cause and been certain of the speed-of-light motion of anything entering the volume.

Why, then, had he said nothing?

One thing is certain. *Nothing* Priss would do at the billiard table could be accidental. He was an expert and the billiard ball did exactly what he wanted it to. I was standing right there. I saw him look at Bloom and then at the table as though he were judging angles.

I watched him hit that ball. I watched it bounce off the side of the table and move into the zero-gravity volume, heading in one particular direction.

For when Priss sent that ball toward the zero-gravity volume – and the tri-di films bear me out – it was *already* aimed directly at Bloom's heart!

Accident? Coincidence?
... Murder?

Afterword

A friend of mine after reading the above story suggested I change the title to 'Dirty Pool'. I have been tempted to do so but have refrained, for it seems too flippant a title for so grave a story – or perhaps I am just corroded with jealousy at not having thought of it first.

But in either case, now that all the stories in this volume have been gone over, and I have experienced the memories to which each gave rise, all I can say is, 'Gee, it's great to be a science fiction writer.'

Silence – and something more than silence. Not only silence, but an absence, a not being there, a vacuum.

The realization came thudding hard into his understanding. He had been abandoned, all ties with him had been cut – in the depth of unguessed space, he had been set adrift. They had washed their hands of him and he was not only naked, but alone.

They knew what had happened. They knew everything that ever happened to him, they monitored him continuously and would know everything he knew. And they had sensed the danger, perhaps even before he, himself, had sensed it. Had recognized the danger, not only to himself, but to themselves as well. If something could get to him, it could trace back the linkage and get to them as well. So the linkage had been cut and would not be restored. They weren't taking any chances. It had been something that had been emphasized time and time again. You must remain not only unrecognized, but entirely unsuspected. You must do nothing that will make you known. You must never point a finger at us.

Cold, callous, indifferent. And frightened. More frightened, perhaps, than he was. For now they knew there was something in the galaxy that could become aware of the disembodied observer they had been sending out. They could never send another, if indeed they had another, for the old fear would be there. And perhaps an even greater fear – based upon the overriding suspicion that the linkage had been cut not quite soon enough, that this factor which had spotted their observer had already traced it back to them.

Fear for their bodies and their profits . . .

Not for their bodies, a voice said inside him. Not their biologic bodies. There are no longer any of your kind who have biologic bodies ...

Then what? he asked.

An extension of their bodies, carrying on the purpose those with bodies gave them in a time when the bodies still existed. Carried on mindlessly ever since, but without a purpose, only with a memory of a purpose ...

Who are you? he asked. How do you know all this? What will you do with me?

In a very different way, it said, I am one like you. You can be like me. You have your freedom now.

I have nothing, he said.

You have yourself, it said. Is that not enough?

But is self enough? he asked.

And did not need an answer.

For self was the basis of all life, all sentience. The institutions, the cultures, the economics were no more than structures for the enhancement of the self. Self now was all he had and self belonged to him. It was all he needed.

Thank you, sir, said he, the last human in the universe.

The Three Laws of Robotics

1. *A robot may not injure a human being, or, through inaction, allow a human being to come to harm.*
2. *A robot must obey the orders given it by human beings except where such orders would conflict with the First Law.*
3. *A robot must protect its own existence as long as such protection does not conflict with the First or Second Laws.*

Lije Baley had just decided to relight his pipe, when the door of his office opened without a preliminary knock, or announcement, of any kind. Baley looked up in pronounced annoyance and then dropped his pipe. It said a good deal for the state of his mind that he let it lie where it had fallen.

'R. Daneel Olivaw,' he said, in a kind of mystified excitement. 'Jehoshaphat! It *is* you, isn't it?'

'You are quite right,' said the tall, bronzed newcomer, his even features never flicking for a moment out of their accustomed calm. 'I regret surprising you by entering without warning, but the situation is a delicate one and there must be as little involvement as possible on the part of the men and robots even in this place. I am, in any case, pleased to see you again, friend Elijah.'

And the robot held out his right hand in a gesture as thoroughly human as was his appearance. It was Baley who was so unmanned by his astonishment as to stare at the hand with a momentary lack of understanding.

But then he seized it in both his, feeling its warm firmness. 'But Daneel, *why*? You're welcome any time, but – What is this situation that is a delicate one? Are we in trouble again? Earth, I mean?'

'No, friend Elijah, it does not concern Earth. The situation to which I refer as a delicate one is, to outward appearances, a small thing. A dispute between mathematicians, nothing more. As we happened, quite by accident, to be within an easy Jump of Earth —'

'This dispute took place on a starship, then?'

'Yes, indeed. A small dispute, yet to the humans involved astonishingly large.'

Baley could not help but smile. 'I'm not surprised you find humans astonishing. They do not obey the Three Laws.'

'That is, indeed, a shortcoming,' said R. Daneel, gravely, 'and I think humans themselves are puzzled by humans. It may be that you are less puzzled than are the men of other worlds because so many more human beings live on Earth than on the Spacer worlds. If so, and I believe it is so, you could help us.'

R. Daneel paused momentarily and then said, perhaps a shade too quickly, 'And yet there are rules of human behavior which I have learned. It would seem, for instance, that I am deficient in etiquette, by human standards, not to have asked after your wife and child.'

'They are doing well. The boy is in college and Jessie is involved in local politics. The amenities are taken care of. Now tell me how you come to be here.'

'As I said, we were within an easy Jump of Earth,' said R. Daneel, 'so I suggested to the captain that we consult you.'

'And the captain agreed?' Baley had a sudden picture of

the proud and autocratic captain of a Spacer starship consenting to make a landing on Earth – of all worlds – and to consult an Earthman – of all people.

'I believe,' said R. Daneel, 'that he was in a position where he would have agreed to anything. In addition, I praised you very highly; although, to be sure, I stated only the truth. Finally, I agreed to conduct all negotiations so that none of the crew, or passengers, would need to enter any of the Earthman cities.'

'And talk to any Earthman, yes. But what has happened?'

'The passengers of the starship, *Eta Carina*, included two mathematicians who were traveling to Aurora to attend an interstellar conference on neurobiophysics. It is about these mathematicians, Alfred Barr Humboldt and Gennao Sabbat, that the dispute centers. Have you perhaps, friend Elijah, heard of one, or both, of them?'

'Neither one,' said Baley, firmly. 'I know nothing about mathematics. Look, Daneel, surely you haven't told anyone I'm a mathematics buff or —'

'Not at all, friend Elijah. I know you are not. Nor does it matter, since the exact nature of the mathematics involved is in no way relevant to the point at issue.'

'Well, then, go on.'

'Since you do not know either man, friend Elijah, let me tell you that Dr. Humboldt is well into his twenty-seventh decade – Pardon me, friend Elijah?'

'Nothing. Nothing,' said Baley, irritably. He had merely muttered to himself, more or less incoherently, in a natural reaction to the extended life-spans of the Spacers. 'And he's still active, despite his age? On Earth, mathematicians after thirty or so . . .'

Daneel said, calmly; 'Dr. Humboldt is one of the top three mathematicians, by long-established repute, in the galaxy. Certainly he is still active. Dr. Sabbat, on the other hand, is quite young, not yet fifty, but he has already established himself as the most remarkable new talent in the most abstruse branches of mathematics.'

'They're both great, then,' said Baley. He remembered his pipe and picked it up. He decided there was no point in lighting it now and knocked out the dottle. 'What happened? Is this a murder case? Did one of them apparently kill the other?'

'Of these two men of great reputation, one is trying to destroy the other. By human values, I believe this may be regarded as worse than physical murder.'

'Sometimes, I suppose. Which one is trying to destroy the other?'

'Why, that, friend Elijah, is precisely the point at issue. Which?'

'Go on.'

'Dr. Humboldt tells the story clearly. Shortly before he boarded the starship, he had an insight into a possible method for analyzing neural pathways from changes in microwave absorption patterns of local cortical areas. The insight was a purely mathematical technique of extraordinary subtlety, but I cannot, of course, either understand or sensibly transmit the details. These do not, however, matter. Dr. Humboldt considered the matter and was more convinced each hour that he had something revolutionary on hand, something that would dwarf all his previous accomplishments in mathematics. Then he discovered that Dr. Sabbat was on board.'

'Ah. And he tried it out on young Sabbat?'

'Exactly. The two had met at professional meetings before and knew each other thoroughly by reputation. Humboldt went into it with Sabbat in great detail. Sabbat backed Humboldt's analysis completely and was unstinting in his praise of the importance of the discovery and of the ingenuity of the discoverer. Heartened and reassured by this, Humboldt prepared a paper outlining, in summary, his work and, two days later, prepared to have it forwarded subetherically to the co-chairmen of the conference at Aurora, in order that he might officially establish his priority and arrange for possible discussion before the sessions were closed. To his surprise, he found that Sabbat was ready with a paper of his own, essentially the same as Humboldt's, and Sabbat was also preparing to have it subetherized to Aurora.'

'I suppose Humboldt was furious.'

'Quite!'

'And Sabbat? What was his story?'

'Precisely the same as Humboldt's. Word for word.'

'Then just what is the problem?'

'Except for the mirror-image exchange of names. According to Sabbat, it was he who had the insight, and he who consulted Humboldt; it was Humboldt who agreed with the analysis and praised it.'

'Then each one claims the idea is his and that the other stole it. It doesn't sound like a problem to me at all. In matters of scholarship, it would seem only necessary to produce the records of research, dated and initialed. Judgment as to priority can be made from that. Even if one is falsified, that might be discovered through internal inconsistencies.'

'Ordinarily, friend Elijah, you would be right, but this is mathematics, and not in an experimental science. Dr. Humboldt claims to have worked out the essentials in his head. Nothing was put in writing until the paper itself was prepared. Dr. Sabbat, of course, says precisely the same.'

'Well, then, be more drastic and get it over with, for sure. Subject each one to a psychic probe and find out which of the two is lying.'

R. Daneel shook his head slowly, 'Friend Elijah, you do not understand these men. They are both of rank and scholarship, Fellows of the Imperial Academy. As such, they cannot be subjected to trial of professional conduct except by a jury of their peers – their professional peers – unless they personally and voluntarily waive that right.'

'Put it to them, then. The guilty man won't waive the right because he can't afford to face the psychic probe. The innocent man will waive it at once. You won't even have to use the probe.'

'It does not work that way, friend Elijah. To waive the right in such a case – to be investigated by laymen – is a serious and perhaps irrecoverable blow to prestige. Both men steadfastly refuse to waive the right to special trial, as a matter of pride. The question of guilt, or innocence, is quite subsidiary.'

'In that case, let it go for now. Put the matter in cold storage until you get to Aurora. At the neurobiophysical conference, there will be a huge supply of professional peers, and then —'

'That would mean a tremendous blow to science itself, friend Elijah. Both men would suffer for having been the instrument of scandal. Even the innocent one would be blamed for having been party to a situation so distasteful. It would be felt that it should have been settled quietly out of court at all costs.'

'All right. I'm not a Spacer, but I'll try to imagine that this attitude makes sense. What do the men in question say?'

'Humboldt agrees thoroughly. He says that if Sabbat will admit theft of the idea and allow Humboldt to proceed with transmission of the paper – or at least its delivery at the conference, he will not press charges. Sabbat's misdeed will remain secret with him; and, of course, with the captain, who is the only other human to be party to the dispute.'

'But young Sabbat will not agree?'

'On the contrary, he agreed with Dr. Humboldt to the last detail – with the reversal of names. Still the mirror-image.'

'So they just sit there, stalemated?'

'Each, I believe, friend Elijah, is waiting for the other to give in and admit guilt.'

'Well, then, wait.'

'The captain has decided that cannot be done. There are two alternatives to waiting, you see. The first is that both will remain stubborn so that when the starship lands on Aurora, the intellectual scandal will break. The captain, who is responsible for justice on board ship will suffer disgrace for not having been able to settle the matter quietly and that, to him, is quite insupportable.'

'And the second alternative?'

'Is that one, or the other, of the mathematicians will indeed admit to wrongdoing. But will the one who confesses do so out of actual guilt, or out of a noble desire to prevent the scandal? Would it be right to deprive of credit one who is sufficiently ethical to prefer to lose that credit than to see science as a whole suffer? Or else, the guilty party will confess at the last moment, and in such a way as to make it appear he does so only for the sake of science, thus escaping the disgrace of his deed and casting its shadow upon the

154

other. The captain will be the only man to know all this but he does not wish to spend the rest of his life wondering whether he has been a party to a grotesque miscarriage of justice.'

Baley sighed. 'A game of intellectual chicken. Who'll break first as Aurora comes nearer and nearer? Is that the whole story now, Daneel?'

'Not quite. There are witnesses to the transaction.'

'Jehoshaphat! Why didn't you say so at once. *What* witnesses?'

'Dr. Humboldt's personal servant —'

'A robot, I suppose.'

'Yes, certainly. He is called R. Preston. This servant, R. Preston, was present during the initial conference and he bears out Dr. Humboldt in every detail.'

'You mean he says that the idea was Dr. Humboldt's to begin with; that Dr. Humboldt detailed it to Dr. Sabbat; that Dr. Sabbat praised the idea, and so on.'

'Yes, in full detail.'

'I see. Does that settle the matter or not? Presumably not.'

'You are quite right. It does not settle the matter, for there is a second witness. Dr. Sabbat also has a personal servant, R. Idda, another robot of, as it happens the same model as R. Preston, made, I believe, in the same year in the same factory. Both have been in service equal times.'

'An odd coincidence – very odd.'

'A fact, I am afraid, and it makes it difficult to arrive at any judgment based on obvious differences between the two servants.'

'R. Idda, then, tells the same story as R. Preston?'

'Precisely the same story, except for the mirror-image reversal of the names.'

'R. Idda stated, then, that young Sabbat, the one not yet fifty' – Lije Baley did not entirely keep the sardonic note out of his voice; he himself was not yet fifty and he felt far from young – 'had the idea to begin with; that he detailed it to Dr. Humboldt, who was loud in his praises, and so on.'

'Yes, friend Elijah.'

155

'And one robot is lying, then.'

'So it would seem.'

'It should be easy to tell which. I imagine even a super-ficial examination by a good roboticist —'

'A roboticist is not enough in this case, friend Elijah. Only a qualified robopsychologist would carry weight enough and experience enough to make a decision in a case of this importance. There is no one so qualified on board ship. Such an examination can be performed only when we reach Aurora —'

'And by then the crud hits the fan. Well, you're here on Earth. We can scare up a robopsychologist, and surely any-thing that happens on Earth will never reach the ears of Aurora and there will be no scandal.'

'Except that neither Dr. Humboldt, nor Dr. Sabbat, will allow his servant to be investigated by a robopsychologist of Earth. The Earthman would have to —' He paused.

Lije Baley said stolidly, 'He'd have to touch the robot.'

'These are old servants, well thought of —'

'And not to be sullied by the touch of Earthman. Then what do you want me to do, damn it?' He paused, grimac-ing. 'I'm sorry, R. Daneel, but I see no reason for your having involved me.'

'I was on the ship on a mission utterly irrelevant to the problem at hand. The captain turned to me because he had to turn to someone. I seemed human enough to talk to, and robot enough to be a safe recipient of confidences. He told me the whole story and asked what I would do. I realized the next Jump could take us as easily to Earth as to our target. I told the captain that, although I was at as much a loss to resolve the mirror-image as he was, there was on Earth one who might help.'

'Jehoshaphat!' muttered Baley under his breath.

'Consider, friend Elijah, that if you succeed in solving this puzzle, it would do your career good and Earth itself might benefit. The matter could not be publicized, of course, but the captain is a man of some influence on his home world and he would be grateful.'

'You just put a greater strain on me.'

156

'I have every confidence,' said R. Daneel, stolidly, 'that you already have some idea as to what procedure ought to be followed.'

'Do you? I suppose that the obvious procedure is to interview the two mathematicians, one of whom would seem to be a thief.'

'I'm afraid, friend Elijah, that neither one will come into the city. Nor would either one be willing to have you come to them.'

'And there is no way of forcing a Spacer to allow contact with an Earthman, no matter what the emergency. Yes, I understand that, Daneel – but I was thinking of an interview by closed-circuit television.'

'Nor that. They will not submit to interrogation by an Earthman.'

'Then what do they want of me? Could I speak to the robots?'

'They would not allow the robots to come here, either.'

'Jehoshaphat, Daneel. *You've* come.'

'That was my own decision. I have permission, while on board ship, to make decisions of that sort without veto by any human being but the captain himself – and he was eager to establish the contact. I, having known you, decided that television contact was insufficient. I wished to shake your hand.'

Lije Baley softened. 'I appreciate that, Daneel, but I still honestly wish you could have refrained from thinking of me at all in this case. Can I talk to the robots by television at least?'

'That, I think, can be arranged.'

'Something, at least. That means I would be doing the work of a robopsychologist – in a crude sort of way.'

'But you are a detective, friend Elijah, not a robopsychologist.'

'Well, let it pass. Now before I see them, let's think a bit. Tell me: is it possible that both robots are telling the truth? Perhaps the conversation between the two mathematicians was equivocal. Perhaps it was of such a nature that each robot could honestly believe its own master was proprietor of the idea. Or perhaps one robot heard only one portion of the discussion and the other another portion, so that each could suppose its own master was proprietor of the idea.'

'That is quite impossible, friend Elijah. Both robots repeat the conversation in identical fashion. And the two repetitions are fundamentally inconsistent.'

'Then it is absolutely certain that one of the robots is lying?'

'Yes.'

'Will I be able to see the transcript of all evidence given so far in the presence of the captain, if I should want to?'

'I thought you would ask that and I have copies with me.'

'Another blessing. Have the robots been cross-examined at all, and is that cross-examination included in the transcript?'

'The robots have merely repeated their tales. Cross-examination would be conducted only by robopsychologists.'

'Or by myself?'

'You are a detective, friend Elijah, not a —'

'All right, R. Daneel. I'll try to get the Spacer psychology straight. A detective can't do it because he isn't a robopsychologist. Let's think further. Ordinarily a robot will not lie, but he will do so if necessary to maintain the Three Laws. He might lie to protect, in legitimate fashion, his own existence in accordance with the Third Law. He is more apt to lie if that is necessary to follow a legitimate order given him by a human being in accordance with the Second Law. He is most apt to lie if that is necessary to save a human life, or to prevent harm from coming to a human in accordance with the First Law.'

'Yes.'

'And in this case, each robot would be defending the professional reputation of his master, and would lie if it were necessary to do so. Under the circumstances, the professional reputation would be nearly equivalent to life and there might be a near-First-Law urgency to the lie.'

'Yet by the lie, each servant would be harming the professional reputation of the other's master, friend Elijah.'

'So it would, but each robot might have a clearer conception of the value of its own master's reputation and honestly

158

judge it to be greater than that of the other's. The lesser harm would be done by his lie, he would suppose, than by the truth.'

Having said that, Lije Baley remained quiet for a moment. Then he said, 'All right, then, can you arrange to have me talk to one of the robots – to R. Idda first, I think?'

'Dr. Sabbat's robot?'

'Yes,' said Baley, dryly, 'the young fellow's robot.'

'It will take me but a few minutes,' said R. Daneel. 'I have a micro-receiver outfitted with a projector. I will need merely a blank wall and I think this one will do if you will allow me to move some of these film cabinets.'

'Go ahead. Will I have to talk into a microphone of some sort?'

'No, you will be able to talk in an ordinary manner. Please pardon me, friend Elijah, for a moment of further delay. I will have to contact the ship and arrange for R. Idda to be interviewed.'

'If that will take some time, Daneel, how about giving me the transcripted material of the evidence so far.'

Lije Baley lit his pipe while R. Daneel set up the equipment, and leafed through the flimsy sheets he had been handed.

The minutes passed and R. Daneel said, 'If you are ready, friend Elijah, R. Idda is. Or would you prefer a few more minutes with the transcript?'

'No,' sighed Baley, 'I'm not learning anything new. Put him on and arrange to have the interview recorded and transcribed.'

R. Idda, unreal in two-dimensional projection against the wall, was basically metallic in structure – not at all the humanoid creature that R. Daneel was. His body was tall but blocky, and there was very little to distinguish him from the many robots Baley had seen, except for minor structural details.

Baley said, 'Greetings, R. Idda.'

'Greetings, sir,' said R. Idda, in a muted voice that sounded surprisingly humanoid.

'You are the personal servant of Gennao Sabbat, are you not?'

'I am, sir.'

'For how long, boy?'

'For twenty-two years, sir.'

'And your master's reputation is valuable to you?'

'Yes, sir.'

'Would you consider it of importance to protect that reputation?'

'Yes, sir.'

'As important to protect his reputation as his physical life?'

'No, sir.'

'As important to protect his reputation as the reputation of another.'

R. Idda hesitated. He said, 'Such cases must be decided on their individual merit, sir. There is no way of establishing a general rule.'

Baley hesitated. These Spacer robots spoke more smoothly and intellectually than Earth-models did. He was not at all sure he could out-think one.

He said, 'If you decided that the reputation of your master were more important than that of another, say, that of Alfred Barr Humboldt, would you lie to protect your master's reputation?'

'I would, sir.'

'Did you lie in your testimony concerning your master in his controversy with Dr. Humboldt?'

'No, sir.'

'But if you were lying, you would deny you were lying in order to protect that lie, wouldn't you?'

'Yes, sir.'

'Well, then,' said Baley, 'let's consider this. Your master, Gennao Sabbat, is a young man of great reputation in mathematics, but he is a young man. If, in this controversy with Dr. Humboldt, he had succumbed to temptation and had acted unethically, he would suffer a certain eclipse of reputation, but he is young and would have ample time to recover. He would have many intellectual triumphs ahead of him and men would eventually look upon this plagiaristic attempt as the mistake of a hot-blooded youth, deficient in judgment. It would be something that would be made up for in the future.

'If, on the other hand, it were Dr. Humboldt who succumbed to temptation, the matter would be much more serious. He is an old man whose great deeds have spread over centuries. His reputation has been unblemished hitherto. All of that, however, would be forgotten in the light of this one crime of his later years, and he would have no opportunity to make up for it in the comparatively short time remaining to him. There would be little more that he could accomplish. There would be so many more years of work ruined in Humboldt's case than in that of your master and so much less opportunity to win back his position. You see, don't you, that Humboldt faces the worse situation and deserves the greater consideration?'

There was a long pause. Then R. Idda said, with unmoved voice, 'My evidence was a lie. It was Dr. Humboldt whose work it was, and my master has attempted, wrongfully, to appropriate the credit.'

Baley said, 'Very well, boy. You are instructed to say nothing to anyone about this until given permission by the captain of the ship. You are excused.'

The screen blanked out and Baley puffed at his pipe. 'Do you suppose the captain heard that, Daneel?'

'I am sure of it. He is the only witness, except for us.'

'Good. Now for the other.'

'But is there any point to that, friend Elijah, in view of what R. Idda has confessed?'

'Of course there is. R. Idda's confession means nothing.'

'Nothing?'

'Nothing at all. I pointed out that Dr. Humboldt's position was the worse. Naturally, if he were lying to protect Sabbat, he would switch to the truth as, in fact, he claimed to have done. On the other hand, if he were telling the truth, he would switch to a lie to protect Humboldt. It's still mirror-image and we haven't gained anything.'

'But then what will we gain by questioning R. Preston?'

'Nothing, if the mirror-image were perfect – but it is not.

After all, one of the robots *is* telling the truth to begin with, and one *is* lying to begin with, and that is a point of asymmetry. Let me see R. Preston. And if the transcription of R. Idda's examination is done, let me have it.'

The projector came into use again. R. Preston stared out of it; identical with R. Idda in every respect, except for some trivial chest design.

Baley said, 'Greetings, R. Preston.' He kept the record of R. Idda's examination before him as he spoke.

'Greetings, sir,' said R. Preston. His voice was identical with that of R. Idda.

'You are the personal servant of Alfred Barr Humboldt, are you not?'

'I am, sir.'

'For how long, boy?'

'For twenty-two years, sir.'

'And your master's reputation is valuable to you?'

'Yes, sir.'

'Would you consider it of importance to protect that reputation?'

'Yes, sir.'

'As important to protect his reputation as his physical life?'

'No, sir.'

'As important to protect his reputation as the reputation of another?'

R. Preston hesitated. He said, 'Such cases must be decided on their individual merit, sir. There is no way of establishing a general rule.'

Baley said, 'If you decided that the reputation of your master were more important than that of another, say, that of Gennao Sabbat, would you lie to protect your master's reputation?'

'I would, sir.'

'Did you lie in your testimony concerning your master in his controversy with Dr. Sabbat?'

'No, sir.'

'But if you were lying, you would deny you were lying, in order to protect that lie, wouldn't you?'

'Yes, sir.'

'Well, then,' said Baley, 'let's consider this. Your master, Alfred Barr Humboldt, is an old man of great reputation in mathematics, but he is an old man. If, in this controversy with Dr. Sabbat, he had succumbed to temptation and had acted unethically, he would suffer a certain eclipse of reputation, but his great age and his centuries of accomplishments would stand against that and would win out. Men would look upon this plagiaristic attempt as the mistake of a perhaps-sick old man, no longer certain in judgment.

'If, on the other hand, it were Dr. Sabbat who had succumbed to temptation, the matter would be much more serious. He is a young man, with a far less secure reputation. He would ordinarily have centuries ahead of him in which he might accumulate knowledge and achieve great things. This will be closed to him, now, obscured by one mistake of his youth. He has a much longer future to lose than your master has. You see, don't you, that Sabbat faces the worse situation and deserves the greater consideration?'

There was a long pause. Then R. Preston said, with unmoved voice, 'My evidence was a l —'

At that point, he broke off and said nothing more.

Baley said, 'Please continue, R. Preston.'

There was no response.

R. Daneel said, 'I am afraid, friend Elijah, that R. Preston is in stasis. He is out of commission.'

'Well, then,' said Baley, 'we have finally produced an asymmetry. From this, we can see who the guilty person is.'

'In what way, friend Elijah?'

'Think it out. Suppose you were a person who had committed no crime and that your personal robot were a witness to that. There would be nothing you need do. Your robot would tell the truth and bear you out. If, however, you were a person who *had* committed the crime, you would have to depend on your robot to lie. That would be a somewhat riskier position, for although the robot would lie, if necessary, the greater inclination would be to tell the truth, so that the lie would be less firm than the truth would be. To prevent that, the crime-committing person would very likely have to *order* the robot to lie. In this way, First Law

163

would be strengthened by Second Law; perhaps very substantially strengthened.'

'That would seem reasonable,' said R. Daneel.

'Suppose we have one robot of each type. One robot would switch from truth, unreinforced, to the lie, and could do so after some hesitation, without serious trouble. The other robot would switch from the lie, *strongly reinforced*, to the truth, but could do so only at the risk of burning out various positronic-trackways in his brain and falling into stasis.'

'And since R. Preston went into stasis —'

'R. Preston's master, D. Humboldt, is the man guilty of plagiarism. If you transmit this to the captain and urge him to face Dr. Humboldt with the matter at once, he may force a confession. If so, I hope you will tell me immediately.'

'I will certainly do so. You will excuse me, friend Elijah? I must talk to the captain privately.'

'Certainly. Use the conference room. It is shielded.'

Baley could do no work of any kind in R. Daneel's absence. He sat in uneasy silence. A great deal would depend on the value of his analysis, and he was acutely aware of his lack of expertise in robotics.

R. Daneel was back in half an hour – very nearly the longest half hour of Baley's life.

There was no use, of course, in trying to determine what had happened from the expression of the humanoid's impassive face. Baley tried to keep his face impassive.

'Yes, R. Daneel?' he asked.

'Precisely as you said, friend Elijah. Dr. Humboldt has confessed. He was counting, he said, on Dr. Sabbat giving way and allowing Dr. Humboldt to have this one last triumph. The crisis is over and you will find the captain grateful. He has given me permission to tell you that he admires your subtlety greatly and I believe that I, myself, will achieve favor for having suggested you.'

'Good,' said Baley, his knees weak and his forehead moist now that his decision had proven correct, 'but Jehoshaphat, R. Daneel, don't put me on the spot like that again, will you?'

'I will try not to, friend Elijah. All will depend, of course, on the importance of a crisis, on your nearness, and on certain other factors. Meanwhile, I have a question —'

'Yes?'

'Was it not possible to suppose that passage from a lie to the truth was easy, while passage from the truth to a lie was difficult? And in that case, would not the robot in stasis have been going from a truth to a lie, and since R. Preston was in stasis, might one not have drawn the conclusion that it was Dr. Humboldt who was innocent and Dr. Sabbat who was guilty?'

'Yes, R. Daneel. It was possible to argue that way, but it was the other argument that proved right. Humboldt did confess, didn't he?'

'He did. But with arguments possible in both directions, how could you, friend Elijah, so quickly pick the correct one?'

For a moment, Baley's lips twitched. Then he relaxed and they curved into a smile. 'Because, R. Daneel, I took into account human reactions, not robotic ones. I know more about human beings than about robots. In other words, I had an idea as to which mathematician was guilty before I ever interviewed the robots. Once I provoked an asymmetric response in them, I simply interpreted it in such a way as to place the guilt on the one I already believed to be guilty. The robotic response was dramatic enough to break down the guilty man; my own analysis of human behavior might not have been sufficient to do so.'

'I am curious to know what your analysis of human behavior was?'

'Jehoshaphat, R. Daneel; think, and you won't have to ask. There is another point of asymmetry in this tale of mirror-image besides the matter of true-and-false. There is the matter of the age of the two mathematicians; one is quite old and one is quite young.'

'Yes, of course, but what then?'

'Why, this. I can see a young man, flushed with a sudden, startling and revolutionary idea, consulting in the matter an old man whom he has, from his early student days, thought of as a demigod in the field. I can *not* see an old man, rich

165

in honors and used to triumphs, coming up with a sudden, startling and revolutionary idea, consulting a man centuries his junior whom he is bound to think of as a young whipper-snapper – or whatever term a Spacer would use. Then, too, if a young man had the chance, would he try to steal the idea of a revered demigod? It would be unthinkable. On the other hand, an old man, conscious of declining powers, might well snatch at one last chance of fame and consider a baby in the field to have no rights he was bound to observe. In short, it was not conceivable that Humboldt consult Sabbat, or that Sabbat steal Humboldt's idea; and from both angles, Dr. Humboldt was guilty.'

R. Daneel considered that for a long time. Then he held out his hand. 'I must leave now, friend Elijah. It was good to see you. May we meet again soon.'

Baley gripped the robot's hand, warmly, 'If you don't mind, R. Daneel,' he said, 'not too soon.'

THE SCIENCE FICTION BOOKS
OF ISAAC ASIMOV

The books are listed in chronological order of publication. The publisher of the first World edition is given, and where this was an American edition this is indicated by (US). Following this, all British editions are listed.

Short stories are indicated by 'collection', Omnibus Editions have a list of contents and these are cross-indexed by the use of In: references. All reissues of a book under a different title are listed with the original title.

Books published in hardcover are indicated by (hd) while all others are paperbacks. The date for each edition is also given. An asterisk (*) indicates that the edition was in print when this list was revised in 1976.

BIBLIOGRAPHY

PEBBLE IN THE SKY
> Doubleday (US hd), 1950; Corgi, 1958; Sidgwick & Jackson (hd), 1968*; Sphere, 1969*.
> In: *Triangle*, 1961.

I, ROBOT (collection)
> Gnome Press (US hd), 1950; Grayson (hd), 1952; Science Fiction Book Club (hd), 1954; Digit, 1958; Dobson (hd), 1967*; Panther, 1968*.

THE STARS, LIKE DUST
> Doubleday (US hd), 1951; Panther, 1958*.
> In: *Triangle*, 1961.
> Title change: *The Rebellious Stars*.
> Ace (US), 1954.

FOUNDATION
> Gnome Press (US hd), 1951; Weidenfeld & Nicolson (hd), 1953; Panther, 1960*.

In: *The Foundation Trilogy*, 1963.
Title change: *The 1,000 Year Plan.*
Ace (US), 1955.

DAVID STARR, SPACE RANGER
Doubleday (Us hd) (as by Paul French), 1952; World's
Work (hd) (as by Paul French), 1953.
Title change: *Space Ranger.*
In: *An Isaac Asimov Double*, 1972.
New English Library, 1973*.

THE CURRENTS OF SPACE
Doubleday (US hd), 1952; Boardman (hd), 1955; Panther,
1958*.
In: *Triangle*, 1961.

FOUNDATION AND EMPIRE
Gnome Press (US hd), 1952; Panther, 1962*.
In: *The Foundation Trilogy*, 1963.
Title change: *The Man Who Upset the Universe*
Ace (US), 1955.

LUCKY STARR AND THE PIRATES OF THE ASTEROIDS
Doubleday (US hd) (as by Paul French), 1953; World's
Work (hd) (as by Paul French), 1954.
Title change: *Pirates of the Asteroids.*
In: *An Isaac Asimov Double*, 1972.
New English Library, 1973*.

SECOND FOUNDATION
Gnome Press (US hd), 1953; Digit, 1958; Panther, 1964*.
In: *The Foundation Trilogy*, 1963.
Title change: *Second Foundation: Galactic Empire.*
Avon (US), 1958.

THE CAVES OF STEEL
Doubleday (US hd), 1954; Boardman (hd), 1954; Science
Fiction Book Club (hd), 1956; Panther, 1958*.
In: *The Rest of the Robots*, 1964.

LUCKY STARR AND THE OCEANS OF VENUS
Doubleday (US hd) (as by Paul French), 1954.
Title change: *Oceans of Venus.*
In: *A Second Isaac Asimov Double*, 1973.
New English Library, 1974.*

THE MARTIAN WAY (collection)
  Doubleday (Us hd), 1955; Dobson (hd), 1964; Panther, 1965*.

THE END OF ETERNITY
  Doubleday (US hd), 1955; Panther, 1959*; Abelard-Schuman (hd), 1975*.

LUCKY STARR AND THE BIG SUN OF MERCURY
  Doubleday (US hd) (as by Paul French), 1956.
  Title change: *The Big Sun of Mercury*.
  In: *The Second Isaac Asimov Double*, 1973.
  New English Library, 1974*.

THE NAKED SUN
  Doubleday (US hd), 1957; Joseph (hd), 1958; Science Fiction Book Club (hd), 1959; Panther, 1960*; White Lion (hd), 1973*.
  In: *The Rest of the Robots*, 1964.

LUCKY STARR AND THE MOONS OF JUPITER
  Doubleday (US hd) (as by Paul French), 1957.
  Title change: *Moons of Jupiter*.
  In: *The Third Isaac Asimov Double*, 1974.
  New English Library, 1974*.

EARTH IS ROOM ENOUGH (collection)
  Doubleday (US hd), 1957; Panther, 1960*; Abelard-Schuman (hd), 1976*.

LUCKY STARR AND THE RINGS OF SATURN
  Doubleday (US hd) (as by Paul French), 1958.
  Title change: *The Rings of Saturn*.
  In: *The Third Isaac Asimov Double*, 1973.
  New English Library, 1974*.

NINE TOMORROWS: TALES OF THE NEAR FUTURE (collection)
  Doubleday (US hd), 1959; Dobson (hd), 1963; Science Fiction Book Club (hd), 1964; Pan, 1966*.

TRIANGLE (collection)
  Doubleday (US hd), 1959.
  Title change: *A Second Isaac Asimov Omnibus*.
  Sidgwick & Jackson (hd), 1969*.
  Contains: *The Currents of Space, Pebble in the Sky* and *The Stars Like Dust*.

THE HUGO WINNERS (anthology edited by Isaac Asimov)
Doubleday (US hd), 1962; Dobson (hd), 1963*; Penguin, 1964.
In: *The Hugo Winners*, 1972.

FIFTY SHORT SCIENCE FICTION TALES (anthology edited by Isaac Asimov and Groff Conclin)
Collier (US), 1963.

THE FOUNDATION TRILOGY (collection)
Doubleday (US hd), 1963.
Title change: *An Isaac Asimov Omnibus.*
Sidgwick & Jackson (hd), 1966*
Contains: *Foundation, Foundation and Empire* and *Second Foundation.*

THE REST OF THE ROBOTS (collection)
Doubleday (US hd), 1964; Dobson (hd), 1967.
Contains: *The Caves of Steel, The Naked Sun* and short stories.
Panther, 1968*.
Contains: short stories only.
Eight Stories from The Rest of the Robots, Pyramid (US), 1966.
Contains: short stories only.
The Robot Novels. Science Fiction Book Club (US hd), 1971.
Contains: *The Caves of Steel* and *The Naked Sun.*

TOMORROW'S CHILDREN: 18 Tales of Fantasy and Science Fiction (anthology edited by Isaac Asimov)
Doubleday (US hd), 1966; Orbit, 1974*.

FANTASTIC VOYAGE
Bantam (US), 1966; Dobson (hd), 1966; Corgi, 1966*.

THROUGH A GLASS CLEARLY (collection)
New English Library, 1967*.

ASIMOV'S MYSTERIES (collection)
Doubleday (US hd), 1968; Rapp & Whiting (hd), 1968; Panther, 1969*.

NIGHTFALL AND OTHER STORIES
Doubleday (US hd), 1969; Rapp & Whiting (hd), 1970.
Nightfall One. Panther, 1971*.
Nightfall Two. Panther, 1971*.

WHERE DO WE GO FROM HERE? (anthology edited by Isaac Asimov)
   Doubleday (US hd), 1971; Joseph (hd), 1973.
   Where Do We Go from Here? Vol. 1. Sphere, 1974*.
   Where Do We Go from Here? Vol. 2. Sphere, 1974*.
THE HUGO WINNERS, VOLUME TWO (anthology edited by Isaac Asimov)
   Doubleday (US hd), 1971.
   The Hugo Winners, Vol. 1. 1963/67. Sphere, 1973.
   The Hugo Winners, Vol. 2. 1968/70. Sphere, 1973.
   In: *The Hugo Winners,* 1973.
THE HUGO WINNERS (anthology edited by Isaac Asimov)
   Science Fiction Book Club (US hd), 1972.
   Contains: *The Hugo Winners* and *The Hugo Winners, Volume Two.*
THE GODS THEMSELVES
   Doubleday (US hd), 1972; Gollancz (hd), 1972*; Panther, 1973*.
THE EARLY ASIMOV, OR, ELEVEN YEARS OF TRYING (collection)
   Doubleday (US hd), 1972; Gollancz (hd), 1973*.
   The Early Asimov, Vol. 1, Panther, 1973*.
   The Early Asimov, Vol. 2, Panther, 1974*.
   The Early Asimov, Vol. 3, Panther, 1974*.
   The Early Asimov, Book 1, Fawcett (US), 1974.
   The Early Asimov, Book 2, Fawcett (US), 1974.
AN ISAAC ASIMOV DOUBLE (collection)
   New English Library (hd), 1972*.
   Contains: *Space Ranger* and *Pirates of the Asteroids.*
A SECOND ISAAC ASIMOV DOUBLE (collection)
   New English Library (hd), 1973*.
   Contains: *The Big Sun of Mercury* and *Oceans of Venus.*
THE THIRD ISAAC ASIMOV DOUBLE (collection)
   New English Library (hd), 1973*.
   Contains: *The Rings of Saturn* and *Moons of Jupiter.*
THE BEST OF ISAAC ASIMOV (collection edited by Angus Wells)
   Sphere, 1973; Sidgwick & Jackson (hd), 1973*.
   The Best of Isaac Asimov: 1939–1952, Sphere, 1975*.

The Best of Isaac Asimov: 1954–1972, Sphere, 1977*.

NEBULA AWARD STORIES 8 (anthology edited by Isaac Asimov)

Harper & Row (US hd), 1973; Gollancz (hd), 1973*; Panther, 1975*.

HAVE YOU SEEN THESE? (collection)

NESFA Press (US hd), 1974.

Expanded as : *Buy Jupiter and Other Stories*, 1975.

BEFORE THE GOLDEN AGE : A SCIENCE FICTION ANTHOLOGY OF THE 1930s (anthology edited by Isaac Asimov)

Doubleday (US hd), 1974; Robson (hd), 1974*; Book Club Associates (hd), 1974.

Before the Golden Age, Vol. 1, Orbit, 1975*.

Before the Golden Age, Vol. 2, Orbit, 1975*.

Before the Golden Age, Vol. 3, Orbit, 1975*.

Before the Golden Age, Vol. 4, Orbit, 1976*.

Before the Golden Age, Book 1, Fawcett (US), 1975.

Before the Golden Age, Book 2, Fawcett (US), 1975.

Before the Golden Age, Book 3, Fawcett (US), 1975.

BUY JUPITER AND OTHER STORIES (collection)

(expanded version of *Have You Seen These?*, 1974).

Doubleday (US hd), 1975; Gollancz (hd), 1976.

More Great Science Fiction Authors from Sphere

THE WORLD OF NULL-A

A. E. VAN VOGT

Gosseyn himself didn't know his own identity – only that he could be killed, yet live again. But someone knew who Gosseyn was, and was using him as a pawn in a deadly game that spanned the galaxy!

0 7221 8757 2   45p

THE PAWNS OF NULL-A

A. E. VAN VOGT

Gosseyn knew the creature threatened to destroy the whole solar system, but not even his Null-A-trained double brain could thwart the Follower's plans. Then he found himself face-to-face with a force that lay at the very roots of human intelligence . . . all the while fighting his own insane mind.

0 7221 8772 6   45p

More Great Science Fiction Authors from Sphere

WAR OF THE WING-MEN

POUL ANDERSON

A sci-fi adventure classic from Hugo Award-winning author Poul Anderson. When three Terrans crash-landed on Diomedes it was clear that their supplies would not carry them across the thousands of miles of unmapped territory to the one Terran outpost. Their only hope was help from the Wing-Men, the barbarian inhabitants of Diomedes.

0 7221 1161 4   60p

THE FALL OF THE TOWERS

SAMUEL R. DELANY

A saga of stunning imaginative power from the winner of three Nebula Awards. The Empire of Toromon was the last hope of mankind after the Great Fire. Sealed off from the radioactive wastelands, the Empire survived to face new and deadly adversaries – the Lord of the Flames, the berserk Imperial military computer, and an invading alien intelligence in search of conquest.

0 7221 2899 1   50p

More Great Science Fiction Authors from Sphere

THE DORSAI TRILOGY

GORDON R. DICKSON

The Hugo Award-winning epic vision of the future, a concept that ranks alongside Asimov's Foundation trilogy in its galaxy-spanning scope.

TACTICS OF MISTAKE

The men of the Dorsai were mercenary troops without equal in the universe. But not even they could anticipate the dramatic effect of Cletus Grahame's brilliant mind and the galaxy-shaking theory he called 'The Tactics of Mistake'. To prove his theory he would risk the future of three worlds and the Dorsai themselves.

0 7221 2954 8   60p

SOLDIER, ASK NOT

On New Earth, the black-clad mercenaries of the Friendly planets pitted their religious fanaticism against the cold courage of the Dorsai. Playing one against the other was Tam Olyn, who, in his search to avenge his dead brother-in-law, was ready to use his frightening knowledge of the Final Encyclopaedia.

0 7221 2952 1   60p

DORSAI!

Donal Graeme, Dorsai of the Dorsai, was the ultimate soldier, a master of space war and strategy. With Donal at their head, the Dorsai embarked upon the final, seemingly impossible venture: unification of the splintered worlds of Mankind.

0 7221 2951 3   50p

All Sphere Books are available at your bookshop or
newsagent, or can be ordered from the following address:
Sphere Books, Cash Sales Department,
P.O. Box 11, Falmouth, Cornwall.

Please send cheque or postal order (no currency), and allow
19p for postage and packing for the first book plus 9p
per copy for each additional book ordered up to a
maximum charge of 73p in U.K.

Customers in Eire and B.F.P.O. please allow 19p for
postage and packing for the first book plus 9p per copy
for the next 6 books, thereafter 3p per book.

Overseas customers please allow 20p for postage and
packing for the first book and 10p per copy for each
additional book.